COOL IT, CARRIE

Carrie sat up straight.

"Okay, so let me get this straight," she said very carefully. "Jordan was the one who stole my story. Not Alex. And everyone knows except *me*. Now why is that?" Her voice rose. "Why does everybody know what happened to *my* story except me?"

Sky didn't know how to respond to that question. Apparently nobody else did, either. The tense silence lasted until the bus turned onto the semicircular drive in front of the school building and screeched to a halt next to the front doors.

Carrie was the first one to get up. She turned to face them.

"I don't know what you guys were thinking," she said. "But if one of you ever wants to . . . wants to . . ." She threw her hands up. "Oh, just forget it!" She whirled and marched down the aisle.

For a long time, nobody moved . . .

M·a·k·i·n·g F·r·i·e·n·d·s

1. Wise up, Alex
2. Cool it, Carrie

Coming soon
3. Face facts, Sky   *November 1997*
4. Grow up, Amy   *December 1997*
5. Go for it, Alex   *January 1998*
6. Tough Luck, Carrie   *February 1998*

All *Making Friends* titles can be ordered at your local bookshop or are available by post from Book Service by Post (tel: 01624 675137).

Making Friends

Cool it, Carrie

Kate Andrews

MACMILLAN CHILDREN'S BOOKS

First published 1997 by Macmillan Children's Books
a division of Macmillan Publishers Limited
25 Eccleston Place, London SW1W 9NF
and Basingstoke

Associated companies throughout the world

ISBN 0 330 35121 4

Copyright © Dan Weiss Associates, Inc. 1997
Photography by Jutta Klee

The right of Kate Andrews to be identified as the
author of this work has been asserted by her in accordance
with the Copyright, Designs and Patents Act 1988.

1 3 5 7 9 8 6 4 2

A CIP catalogue record for this book is available from
the British Library

Printed and bound in Great Britain by Mackays of Chatham plc, Kent

The cast of
M·a·k·i·n·g F·r·i·e·n·d·s

Alex

Age: 13

Looks: Light brown hair, blue eyes

Family: Mother died when she was a baby; lives with her dad and her brother Matt, aged 14

Likes: Skateboarding; her family and friends; wearing baggy T-shirts and jeans; being adventurous; letting her feelings show!

Dislikes: People who make fun of her skateboard, her brother or her dad; dressing smart or girly; anything to do with maths or science; dishonesty

Carrie

Age: 13

Looks: Long dark hair – often dyed black! Hazel eyes

Family: Awful! No brothers or sisters; very rich parents who go on about money all the time

Likes: Writing stories; wearing black (drives her mum mad!); thinking deep thoughts; Sky's parents and their awesome houseboat!

Dislikes: Her full name – Carrington; her parents; her mum's choice of clothes; jokes about her hair; computers

Sky

Age: 13

Looks: Light brown skin, dark hair, brown eyes

Family: Crazy! Lives on a houseboat with weird parents and a brother, Leif, aged 8

Likes: Shopping; trendy gear; TV; pop music; talking!

Dislikes: Her parents' bizarre lifestyle; having no money; eating meat

Jordan

Age: 13

Looks: Floppy fair hair, green eyes

Family: Uncomfortable! Four big brothers – all so brilliant at sports he can never compete with them

Likes: Drawing! (especially cartoons); basketball (but don't tell anyone!); playing sax (badly); taking the mickey out of his brothers

Dislikes: Being "baby brother" to four brainless apes; Sky when she starts gossiping

Sam

Age: 13

Looks: Native-American; very dark hair, very dark eyes

Family: Confusing! Both parents are Native-American but have different views on how their kids should look and behave; one sister – Shawna, aged 16

Likes: Skateboarding with Alex; computers (especially surfing the Net); writing for the school paper; goofing around

Dislikes: The way his friends dump their problems on each other; his parents' arguments

Amy

Age: 13

Looks: Sickeningly gorgeous blonde hair; baby blue eyes (yuck!)

Family: Spoilt rotten by her dad, which worries her mum; two big sisters

Likes: Having loads of expensive clothes; making other people feel stupid; Matt (Alex's brother) – she fancies him; being leader of "The Amys" – her bunch of snobby friends

Dislikes: Alex, Carrie and Sky! Looking stupid or childish

Mel

Age: 13

Looks: Black hair, dark eyes

Family: Nice parents who work very hard to do their best for Mel

Likes: Her mum and dad; her friends – but should these be the Amys, or Alex, Carrie and Sky? Standing up for herself; reading horror novels

Dislikes: Amy, when she's rotten to other people; worrying about who are her *real* friends

The Three Girls Who Lived on the Hill

A monstrous tale of twisted evil
By Carrie Mersel

(Note to myself: Throw original story in trash compactor)

. . . She tried to scream, but the thick smoke left her gasping for air. She tried to run, but it was as if her feet were nailed in place. Mercedes closed her eyes, but there was no escape. The fire was roaring hot. Flames licked at the tasteful drapes that framed the picture window.

Mercedes forced her eyes open. Beyond the flames, the giant white house up on the hillside shimmered through the haze. She knew that inside the house there was a black-and-white checkerboard floor. She knew a lot of things about the house even though she had never been inside.

The heat of the fire intensified. Mercedes stared, mesmerized at the dancing flames as they drew closer and closer—then disappeared entirely.

Mercedes blinked. She was in her own house, sitting on the couch with her two best friends, Suzanne and Alice. They were staring at her intently.

"Why do you keep staring out the window?" Alice asked.

"Are you watching to see if one of them comes out of the mansion?" Suzanne wondered.

The three girls gazed at the huge white building on the top of the hill. It was the biggest, most beautiful house in all of Stony Brook. And it was owned by three of the most beautiful, glamorous, and popular girls in the whole town.

Mercedes wasn't friends with Alexis, Krystle, and Fallon. And she didn't want to be. But everyone else in the town loved the three mysterious girls the same way they loved movie stars. Everyone fought to be invited to the elegant parties at the white mansion on the hill.

"I wonder what they're doing right now," Suzanne said dreamily.

"Probably the same thing we are," Alice said. "I bet they're just like us."

Mercedes started to feel dizzy. Her friends' voices faded into the distance. Her vision blurred, then cleared. She saw two girls, bound and gagged, standing in front of a roaring fire. Sweat broke out on her brow as she strained to see their faces. Slowly the girls began to turn around . . . and then the vision faded.

Mercedes struggled to remain calm. She'd been having these psychic flashes for months—ever since the three girls had moved into the house on the top of the hill. She was certain they were connected. But who would believe her? She had tried to tell Suzanne and Alice once. They had told her she was crazy. They couldn't see anything wrong with the girls who lived on the hill. They couldn't see the danger. . . .

One

Carrie stopped reading out loud. She glanced around the lunch table.

Nobody was listening. Nobody was even looking at her. Sam Wells and Sky Foley were staring at Alex Wagner, who was staring back at them with her mouth hanging open. Finally, Alex swallowed and spared them all the view of the chicken pot pie she was having for lunch.

Carrie hung her head. This was just perfect. Here she was, sharing a private, personal short story with three of her best friends—something she *never* did—and they were trying to gross each other out.

"Do you mind?" she demanded.

Alex shook her head. "Sorry," she finally managed. She brushed her straight brown hair out of her eyes, then took a deep breath and leaned back in her chair. "I was so into your story that I totally forgot I was even eating."

Carrie blushed. So maybe they were paying attention to her story.

"Where did you come *up* with all that stuff?" Sky breathed. She had this wide-eyed, awestruck look on her face. "It's incredible. Seriously. I'm like, totally impressed."

Carrie shrugged, but now she was starting to feel embarrassed. The story wasn't *that* good, was it?

Alex nodded. "You should get up and read it for the whole lunchroom."

Carrie cocked an eyebrow. "And get bombarded with Jell-O cubes?" she asked. "No thanks."

In spite of all the praise, Carrie was fully aware that no one besides her friends would be remotely interested in anything she wrote. *Especially* at lunch. Everyone was too busy shoveling chicken pot pie into their faces and talking with their mouths full.

"Nobody would bombard you with anything," Sam said. Then he grinned mischievously. "Except maybe Alexis, Krystle, and Fallon. I mean . . . The Amys."

"Shh," Carrie whispered. She shot a quick glance over her shoulder at Amy Anderson, Mel Eng, and Aimee Stewart. Luckily they

5

hadn't heard. They were leaning over their table and whispering to one another.

The Amys were the most popular girls at Robert Lowell Middle School. It was like they had the power to determine if you were cool or not. And, for some reason, they had decided Carrie was definitely uncool. The last thing she wanted to do was to make The Amys mad. They were mad enough already. They still hadn't gotten her back for the embarrassing photo of Amy dressed as a Carrie Mersel Wanna-be that Carrie, Alex, and Sky had taped to Amy Anderson's locker last week. But Carrie knew The Amys would have their revenge, sooner or later. It was only Monday.

"Where did you get those names, anyway?" Sam asked.

"They're characters on *Dynasty*," Carrie answered in a low voice.

Sam exchanged a quick, knowing look with Alex and Sam. "Of course," he said.

"Perfect, right?" Carrie asked. She knew that the three of them would understand. *Dynasty* was Carrie's parents' favorite TV show. It had been canceled ages ago. It wasn't even in reruns anymore. But

Carrie's parents had collected a complete video library of all the episodes, which they were constantly trying to get her to watch with them. Even worse, the show had spawned Carrie's own hideous name, which was Carrington.

"Uh . . . can I ask you something, Carrie?" Sky said. She began twirling some of her long, curly brown hair around her forefinger. "See, what I wanted to know is . . . am I supposed to be Alice or Suzanne? I kind of like the name Suzanne better."

"Neither. It's a made-up story. The beginning is only very loosely based on a couple of things." But even as Carrie spoke, she knew she didn't sound very convincing. She couldn't seem to wipe the stupid smile off her face that had appeared once they had started complimenting her.

"Uh . . . loosely?" Alex asked, raising her eyebrows. "I'm not so sure about that. Sounds pretty exact to me." She smirked. "Except the psychic powers and the fact that I do *not* think there's something wrong with you."

"But it's not *you*," Carrie protested. "I mean, Alice isn't riding a skateboard or

7

wearing a green baseball hat, right? Besides, when you hear the end—"

"So I *am* Suzanne," Sky said with a satisfied nod. She took a bite out of her homemade tofu sandwich. "Good."

Carrie sighed. Why was it that none of them could accept the fact that her story had nothing to do with real life? Well, maybe the first part had a little to do with real life. Actually, the first part had a lot to do with real life—but that wasn't the point. The point was that it was a work of fiction.

"Nobody's *anybody*," she said. "I mean— *I'm* not Mercedes. There's nothing in there about Mercedes having dyed black hair. Any resemblance between actual persons living or dead is purely coincidental."

"Hey—how come Jordan and I aren't in the story?" Sam asked, pretending to be offended. "Everybody else is."

Sky suddenly sat up straight and looked around. "Where is Jor-*dumb*, anyway?"

Carrie rolled her eyes. Sometimes the stuff that went on between Sky and Jordan Sullivan was like a bad song that was overplayed on a Top 40 radio station. Jordan would make fun of Sky for something silly, like how she smuggled her own homemade vegetarian lunches into the cafeteria, and Sky would answer by calling him Jor-*dumb*. Their routine had been funny when they were all ten-year-olds, but by now it was pretty stale. Carrie could practically mouth their conversations along with them.

"He's at a dentist appointment," Sam answered.

Sky shook her head. "Man," she said. "I've got to remember to ask my parents to schedule *my* dentist appointments in the middle of a school day, too."

"Look, Carrie," Alex said, pushing aside her half eaten plate of chicken pot pie and leaning across the table. "I'm serious about what I said just now."

Carrie blinked. "About what? That you don't think there's something wrong with me?"

Alex laughed. "No, dummy," she said gently. "About how you should read the story for other people. Why don't you give it to the school newspaper? Maybe you could even try to publish it in a magazine or something."

"Yeah, right," Carrie mumbled. "Like I'm really going to go to the school newspaper and show them *this*. The Amys work on the school newspaper, remember?"

Alex grinned. "I thought you said the story doesn't have anything to do with real life."

"It *doesn't*," Carrie said, but she had to laugh, too. "It's just, you know, certain people might get the wrong idea."

"Well, why don't you submit it under a . . ." Alex snapped her fingers. "What's the word— you know, one of those false names . . ."

"Pseudonym?" Carrie suggested.

Alex's face brightened. "Exactly."

"Because I'm not going to submit it *anywhere* under *any* name," Carrie said firmly. "And that's that."

"*You* wouldn't even have to do it," Alex prodded. "One of us could do it for you."

Hmm. Something about Alex's tone was starting to make Carrie a little nervous. It was the tone Alex always got when she was sure she had a brilliant idea. When Alex was sure she had a brilliant idea, she could be pretty stubborn—almost as stubborn as Carrie, in fact.

"We could even do it right now, before recess," Alex continued excitedly. "I can slip it into the newspaper's mailbox on my way out to the courtyard—"

Carrie held up her hands. "Hold on a second here. I have something important to say. And I'm only going to say it once."

She took a deep breath.

"Nobody—and I mean *nobody*—is going to give anything I've written to *anyone*," she announced. "Nobody at this table is even going to tell anyone else that I *write*. Got it? Because if you do, I'll be forced to kill you." She smiled. "Seriously. And if I do that, I have to go to jail. I don't want to go to jail. The food in jail is probably even worse than the food *here*."

Alex laughed once. "Come on, Carrie—"

"No, really, Alex," Carrie said quietly. "Writing is something I do for myself."

Alex sighed. "Well, that's too bad. 'Cause you've got serious talent."

"Thanks," Carrie mumbled. She shoved the story into the front pocket of her black knapsack. She knew she was blushing again. But even though writing *was* something she did for herself, that was only part of the truth.

The other part—the *secret* part—was

11

that she was petrified. She was petrified that she would humiliate herself. She was petrified that someone would read her story, rip it into neat little shreds, then write a note that went something like this:

```
Dear Ms. Mersel (if that is your
real name),
    Your story was, well . . . let's
just say it was very neatly typed.
Maybe you should think about
pursuing another interest all
together. Something less literary.
Have you thought about garbage
collecting?
    Sincerely,
    Somebody who thinks you're lame
```

Carrie zipped up the pocket on her backpack and patted her story protectively. It had taken her almost a week to get up the nerve to read it to her best friends—friends who knew her really, really well—friends she could trust. *No way* would she ever expose herself to the humiliation of having total strangers read her stories.

Two

As far as Jordan Sullivan was concerned, today had been the ideal school day. The only class he'd attended had been a double period of art, which he had naturally spent goofing off and drawing cartoons. And as soon as that was over, his mother had whisked him off to the dentist. Normally, he hated the dentist. But today he'd had two teeth pulled, so he got to miss the rest of his classes.

Now the day was over and he was feeling all better—just in time for a cookout at the Wagners' house. He and Matt were standing in the driveway of the Wagners' white frame house, shooting hoops at the little basket nailed above the garage door. He figured if the rest of his school days could be like this, his eighth-grade year would be just about perfect. He'd only have to eat a lot of sugar and stop brushing his teeth.

"So how's the world of big-time high

school basketball treating you, anyway?" Jordan asked. "Are you gonna be starting at center or what?"

"I'm not sure yet," Matt said, dribbling between one hand and the other. "It's between me and this other guy. And he's way taller than me. No one's going to be able to stop him from getting to the basket."

"Dinner's almost ready!" Alex called from inside the house. "Can you give me a hand?"

Jordan squinted at the front door. The late afternoon sun was perched behind the pine trees at the end of Yesler Street, glistening off the distant waves of Puget Sound and casting everything in a reddish gold glow. He glanced back at Matt. "Uh . . . you think we should go in and help?" he asked.

"Nah," Matt said. He dribbled a few more times, smirking. "What's that old saying? Too many cooks spoil the burgers."

Alex poked her head out the door. "I heard that, dork boy," she called to her brother. She pulled the bill of her green cap low over her eyes and beckoned to Jordan. "Come here. I need help in the kitchen."

"One last shot." Jordan clapped his hands and waved for a pass. Matt tossed the basketball to him as he backpedaled toward the door. "Sullivan takes the inbounds pass with one second left!" he cried. He spun the ball in his hands and threw up a shot. "He shoots . . ."

The ball fell through the net with a swish.

"He scores! The crowd goes wild!" Jordan began dancing around, waving his arms above his head. "Sullivan wins the NBA championship for the Supersonics!"

Matt and Alex exchanged a grin. "You should try out for the Robert Lowell team," Matt told Jordan.

Jordan stopped dancing. He retrieved the basketball, lobbed it into the garage, and followed Alex into the house. "You know, sometimes I even amaze myself," he chuckled.

"Oh, *please*," Alex groaned. "If you're so amazing, why *haven't* you tried out for the basketball team?"

"Because I want to keep my hoop skills a secret from the rest of my family," he answered.

"Sure you do," Alex said sarcastically.

"No, it's true," he said—and he meant it. Jordan loved basketball, but not nearly as much as he loved being different from his three older meat-for-brains brothers. That was why he didn't play team sports, why he spent most of his free time drawing cartoons, and why he had taken up the saxophone— which was probably the loudest, most annoying musical instrument ever invented. It was perfect for driving his brothers crazy.

Alex shook her head as they entered the Wagners' cozy, old-fashioned kitchen. "Man, what's *with* all you guys?" she asked. "Everybody wants to keep everything that they do well a secret. I think I'm the only show-off left in all of Taylor Haven."

Jordan frowned. "What do you mean, 'you guys'?"

"You with your basketball, and Carrie with her writing," Alex said.

"What about Carrie's writing?" Jordan asked. The two of them slumped down at the table in front of a huge plastic bowl of potato salad. Alex began to stir the thick glop with two big wooden spoons. The smoky odor of grilled hamburger meat drifted through an open window. Jordan's mouth started watering. He'd hardly eaten all day.

"Today at lunch, Carrie read us the first

16

part of this story she's writing," Alex explained. "And when—"

"Whoa, whoa," Jordan interrupted. "She did *what?*"

Alex lifted her shoulders. "She read us this story she's writing that's supposedly 'loosely' based on what happened with The Amys last week," she continued. "Anyway, it was totally amazing. I told her she should show it to somebody or try to sell it . . . or *something.* But she told me I was nuts." She laughed once. "In so many words."

Jordan slouched back in his chair. "I can't *believe* it."

What were the chances of *that* ever happening again? Carrie *never* read anything she wrote out loud. It was one of those unalterable laws of the universe, like the Law of Jordan Sullivan. The Law of Jordan Sullivan stated that with every good thing that happens, two bad things must follow. He shook his head. Well, of course—*that* was why Carrie had read her story out loud. His day had been *too* perfect. He had to miss out on something.

"Well you can still *read* it," Alex said. She gestured toward the counter behind him.

"It's right in the front pocket of her bag."

Jordan turned around. Sure enough, Carrie's black knapsack was sitting right there. He leaned forward and yanked open the zipper, then shoved his hand into the front pocket and pulled out several sheets of folded white paper.

"'The Three Girls Who Lived on the Hill,'" Jordan read aloud as he unfolded the papers on the table. " 'A monstrous tale of—' "

"Alex!" Mr. Wagner yelled from the backyard, cutting Jordan off. "We're almost ready out here!"

"Coming!" Alex called. She snatched up the vat of potato salad in both hands and scrambled for the back door. "Hey, Jordan—grab some napkins and paper plates and stuff on your way out, okay?"

Jordan nodded distractedly. His eyes flashed over the page. Well, there was too much here to read right now—and besides, he was too hungry. He'd just take it home with him and read it on his own time. Carrie wouldn't mind, would she? Nah. After one last look, he folded up the story and crammed it into the back pocket of his jeans.

Right now, it was time to get busy making some more cavities.

Skyler Foley's
Antibarbecue Statement

I'm sorry, but I have just one thing to say about barbecues.

<u>Eww.</u>

Seriously. The idea of people hanging out just to roast up a bunch of meat is maybe the grossest thing in the world. Where did that tradition even start? It probably goes back to the Middle Ages, when big hairy guys with yellow teeth would eat boars and then die of heart attacks at the age of thirty.

Well, society has come a long way since then. I mean, now people can actually go to jail if they don't recycle. That's what I call progress.

The point is that it's high time for the rest of the world to catch up. Meat eating should be a thing of the past, like wide-collared paisley shirts and love beads. (Somebody should tell my parents that, by the way. They still think it's the seventies, but that's a whole other story.) So the next time Mr. Wagner invites everyone over for a barbecue, I'm going to suggest that we have a vegetarian potluck instead.

Of course, the barbecue <u>was</u> a lot of fun. It was especially fun watching Matt kick Jordan's butt at basketball. And Mr. Wagner <u>did</u> go out of his way to buy me veggie burgers, which was very, very cool. Besides, it's not like I want to spoil everyone else's fun, either.

Oh, well. I guess it's kind of hard being a preachy thirteen-year-old vegetarian, isn't it?

Three

By the time Sky and Carrie had made their way from Yesler Street to Carrie's house on Whidbey Road, night had already fallen. Sky shivered. The closer you got to Puget Sound, the more the air felt like the inside of a freezer, especially at night.

"You sure you don't want a ride?" Carrie asked. She paused outside the front door. "It's pretty chilly. Besides, my mom always freaks when she finds out you've been walking home alone at night."

"No, that's all right," Sky said, wrapping her sweater tightly around herself. "It's so pretty out." She gazed up at the clear, star-filled sky. Sky never understood *why* Mrs. Mersel made such a fuss about how she walked home by herself down the little stretch of Pike's Way.

"I wonder where I put my keys," Carrie whispered, fishing around the pocket of her long black skirt. "I don't want to have to ring the doorbell and tear my mom away from some crucial rerun on Nickelodeon."

Sky laughed. Carrie was *way* too hard on her mom, as far as Sky was concerned. So what if Mrs. Mersel watched a lot of TV? Big deal. At least she behaved like a normal adult. That was a lot more than Sky could say about her own parents. They were probably dancing around the main cabin of the houseboat right now to some twenty-year-old song by the Grateful Dead.

"I know they're in here somewhere," Carrie muttered.

Sky let out a deep breath. Even though she would never admit it, she always felt a vague twinge of envy every time she stood in or around the Mersels' big, sleek white house. And she knew perfectly well why. Carrie lived less than half a mile away from the Foleys' dingy little houseboat, but in some ways the two homes couldn't have been further apart.

"Maybe your keys are in your book bag," Sky suggested.

"Maybe," Carrie said doubtfully. She slung her book bag off her shoulder and onto the ground.

Then she froze. Her eyes widened. "Oh no," she gasped.

"What is it?" Sky asked worriedly.

"I don't believe it!" Carrie's hand shot into the front pocket of her book bag. She gazed up at Sky with an expression of utter horror. "My story!" she cried. "It's gone!"

Sky drew in her breath sharply. *Uh-oh.*

"Did you see it anywhere?" Carrie demanded.

Sky shook her head. She knew it was best to keep quiet. Carrie was clearly on her way to a serious freak-out, and Sky had an unfortunate talent for saying the wrong thing in situations like this. Especially with Carrie.

"It's gotta be here somewhere," Carrie breathed in a shaky voice. She crouched down by her book bag and began to tear through every last part of it, tossing her schoolbooks and notebooks onto the front steps as if they were pieces of garbage. "I only have that one copy. I had it this afternoon. . . ."

Instinctively, Sky bent down and began to gather up Carrie's things. *Calm down, Carrie,* she pleaded silently. *Just relax. It'll turn up.*

But Carrie continued to feverishly rifle

through her bag. Finally, when she had emptied it of every last pen cap and piece of lint and scrap of paper, she looked Sky in the eye.

"Are you *sure* you didn't see it anywhere?" she asked desperately. "You didn't see it at Alex's house?"

Sky shook her head once again.

"I—I—I just don't get it," Carrie stuttered. "Somebody must have taken it out of the bag. Could it have been Alex? I mean, I *know* I had it when I got to her house. At least, I'm pretty sure—"

"Carrie, there's no way Alex would have taken your story out of your bag without telling you," Sky interrupted gently. "I mean, you were pretty clear at lunch today when you said you would kill anyone who did anything with—"

Suddenly, the front door flew open.

Sky swallowed.

Mrs. Mersel was towering over them, with her arms folded across her chest and her jaw tightly set. She was also wearing this fancy, perfectly pressed business suit, which made her look even *more* intimidating.

"What's going on out here?" Mrs.

Mersel hissed. "Why are you two making so much noise?"

"Mom, I have to go back to Alex's house." Carrie's voice had a frantic edge to it. "Will you give me a ride?"

"Carrington Mersel, you're not going anywhere." Her mother gestured into the house. "Except inside to do your homework."

"Please, it's really important." Carrie bit her lip. "I brought this story I wrote to school today to show it to everyone, and then I stuck it in my book bag, but when I brought it to Alex's house after school, it must have gotten lost—"

"I assume you typed this story on your typewriter?" Mrs. Mersel interrupted.

Carrie didn't say anything for a moment. "Mom, what on earth does *that* have to do with anything at all?" she asked.

Mrs. Mersel sighed disappointedly. "If you had used a computer, Carrie, this never would have happened. You would have had a backup file. You could have lost a *hundred* copies of this story, and you'd still be able to print out another."

Sky cringed. Carrie's mom didn't seem to see how upset Carrie was. That was a pretty harsh thing to say—especially to somebody who had just lost something so important. In fact, that was about the last thing Carrie needed to hear right now. Carrie *despised* computers.

"Look, just forget it," Carrie moaned. She began shoving all her belongings back into her book bag. "It doesn't even matter."

Mrs. Mersel shook her head. "Come on, Skyler," she said. "I'll give you a ride home."

Sky stood up straight. "Carrie, call Alex, okay?" she murmured as reassuringly as she could. "Maybe it'll turn up at her house."

"Maybe," Carrie said sadly. Obviously *she* didn't have much faith in that possibility, either.

Mrs. Mersel strode down the front walk toward the driveway. "Let's go, Skyler."

Sky cast one last glance at Carrie. She wanted to say something—one last "I'm sure it's not gone" or "Don't worry, you'll find it."

But she didn't.

She knew it wouldn't have done any good, anyway.

Alex Wagner's Book of Deep Thoughts

Entry 5

I have a feeling that this is going to be another very, very interesting week.

And why? Well, because there we were—Matt, my dad, and me—cleaning up after the barbecue, joking around, having a good time . . . when the phone rang. It was Carrie. She was really, really upset. At first she was talking so fast that I couldn't even understand what she was saying. Finally, she managed to slow down enough to tell me that someone had stolen her story.

Namely _me_.

When I finally understood what she was getting at, I have to admit, I was kind of . . . well, mad. Why would she automatically assume that _I_ was the one who stole her story? Why would she even assume that her story was stolen in the first place? But I didn't want to say anything to make her more upset. I <u>would</u> feel really terrible if it was lost. I know how much that story means to her.

The thing is, I'm pretty sure it isn't. In fact, I'm pretty sure I know where it is.

If it's anywhere, it's with Jordan. He was the last one who had it, and knowing him, he probably just shoved it in his pocket and forgot about it. He can be pretty spacey.

Of course, I didn't tell Carrie that. That's because I was worried that if I did, she would call Jordan and totally freak out on him.

See, Carrie is one of my very best friends, but occasionally she gets a little riled up. It doesn't happen very often. Normally, she just lets bad things roll right past her. She always manages to see something funny in a lame situation. In fact, she usually manages to make most lame situations a whole lot better.

But she also has a limit.

So that's why I'm going to talk to Jordan, one-on-one. If he has the story, I can just tell him to slip it into Carrie's locker tomorrow when she isn't looking. That way, Carrie will get her story back, Jordan won't get the third degree, and everything will be back to normal.

It's a pretty brilliant idea, if I do say so myself. Well, unless Jordan doesn't have her story. Then I don't know what will happen. To be honest, I don't really want to think about it, either.

Four

Jordan couldn't believe his luck. He had been expecting to go straight home after the Wagners' barbecue. But his father had left something at the office. And whatever it was, it was something he absolutely *had* to have, since he was leaving on a business trip early the next morning. So when he had picked Jordan up, the two of them had gone on a surprise half-hour drive into downtown Seattle.

The best part about it was that Jordan's father actually felt *guilty* for dragging Jordan along with him. Jordan didn't mind—but having been the youngest child for thirteen years, he knew perfectly well that his father's guilt could be used to his own personal advantage. And since the office just happened to be next to this awesome bookstore that had about a billion comic books, well . . . it wouldn't be *that* bad if Jordan hung out there while his father rummaged around for his missing papers, would it?

And that was that.

So here he was, standing in front of a rack of comic books pretty much the size of his whole house. At nine o'clock. On a school night. It was unreal.

"Jordan?"

What? Jordan looked over his shoulder. He couldn't believe it. His father was already back. So much for enjoying himself. The guy had only been gone for like thirty seconds. Jordan had barely had time to even *look* at anything, much less buy anything.

"Hey, Dad," he asked. "Can't I just have a few more minutes to—"

"Come on, Jordan," his father interrupted. He was grinning that don't-even-try-it grin of his.

"Okay—*one* more minute?" Jordan suggested, smiling hopefully.

Mr. Sullivan shook his head. "Let's go, Jordan."

But right at that moment, something on the door caught Jordan's eye.

ATTENTION YOUNG WRITERS!
The Cheshire Cat Bookstore
is holding a fiction contest.

If you are in high school and have a short story of 3,000 words
or less that you'd like to share with us, please let us know. The
winner will receive a gift certificate of one hundred dollars, good
for any purchase at any Cheshire Cat Bookstore. In addition, this
branch will sponsor a reading of the winner's work this coming
Sunday. The deadline for submissions is Tuesday.

All entries are welcome!
If interested, please ask for George.

Jordan froze.

Wait a second. Today was Tuesday. And
he actually *had* a short story in his back
pocket right now. . . .

"Come *on*," Mr. Sullivan commanded
impatiently.

"Uh—hold on, just . . . just one second,
Dad," Jordan stammered.

He fished the crumpled sheets of paper
out of his jeans and smoothed them flat.
His mind was whirling. Should he hand in
Carrie's story? Alex had said it was really
good. And Carrie would be totally psyched
if she won. But what if she didn't? Jordan

31

knew Carrie was hypersensitive about her writing.

"Jordan!"

Jordan glanced frantically at his father, who was already halfway out the door. He had to make a decision—now. Jordan stared at the sheets of paper in his hand and concentrated. What was the worst that could happen? If he submitted the story and Carrie lost, she wouldn't even know. He could just keep it a secret from her until he found out. And if she *won*—well, then, that would be amazing. Maybe Carrie would even split the prize money with him.

Then he could come back and buy as many comic books as he wanted.

Jordan made his decision. Opportunities like this didn't pop up every single day of the year. It was almost *too* perfect. . . . It was fate.

"Jordan, what are you *doing?*" Mr. Sullivan moaned.

But Jordan was already dashing back into the store. "I'll be right back!" he shouted over his shoulder. He looked around wildly—then at last caught a glimpse of a scruffy-looking sales clerk with a beard and a ponytail behind a stack of bookshelves. The guy didn't look much older than Jordan's eighteen-year-old twin brothers. Jordan dashed up to him. Sure enough, the plastic name tag on the guy's shirt said George.

"Can I help you with something?" George asked.

Jordan nodded, panting. "I have a story I'd like to submit for the fiction contest."

George laughed. "You? Sorry, kid—but you don't look old enough to be in high school."

Jordan reached into his pocket. "Well, actually, it's not *me*," he admitted. He waved the wrinkled papers out in front of him. "It's a friend of mine."

"Hmm." George raised his eyebrows dubiously, but he took the story and glanced at the first page. "Carrie Mersel?"

Jordan nodded vigorously. "That's her."

George glanced at him. "And *she's* in high school."

Jordan chewed on his lip for a moment. Should he lie and say that she was? If he did, she might be disqualified or something if the bookstore found out. "Well, not exactly . . ."

George started laughing again. "Not exactly?"

"Look, she's in eighth grade," Jordan admitted. "But she's an amazing writer. Seriously. Can you just do a me a favor and enter it in the contest?"

"And why should I do *you* any favors?" George asked jokingly.

Jordan shrugged as innocently as he could. "Because you seem like a nice guy, George. And I know you wouldn't want my friend to miss her chance at winning the contest."

"Well . . ."

"*Please*," Jordan begged.

George sighed after a moment. "All right." He handed the story back to Jordan. "Just write her phone number at the top here."

"Thanks a lot, man," Jordan said, scribbling down Carrie's number. "You won't regret this."

Wednesday:
Secrets and Lies

8:43 A.M. For the last time, Carrie asks if anyone has seen her story. But apparently no one has seen it—not Sky, Sam, Jordan, *or* Alex. Carrie buries her face in her hands. So her one copy is really gone forever.

9:35 A.M. Alex corners Jordan alone outside the boys' lockers and demands to know if he was telling the truth to Carrie. Jordan admits to Alex that he *did* take the story. Not only did he take it . . . but he sort of entered it in a fiction contest. Besides, won't Carrie be psyched if she wins?

12:31 P.M. Carrie announces to the lunch table that she's formed a theory as to the whereabouts of the missing story. She's certain that The Amys are responsible. They must have seen her reading it at lunch yesterday, then snatched it out of her book bag on the bus ride home.

Jordan nervously tells Carrie that she's becoming paranoid—like that guy on the *X-Files.* Carrie sticks her tongue out at him.

12:52 P.M. In a moment of guilt, Jordan confesses the truth to Sam. He had no idea Carrie would be so upset. Sam just shakes his head. Basically, it comes down to this: If Carrie finds out that Jordan did something with her story, Jordan should consider moving to another country.

1:45 P.M. Alex and Sky are in Ms. Lloyd's English class. Alex feels as if she's about to burst. Finally, she can't take it anymore. She passes a note to Sky:

Jordan took Carrie's story. He made me promise not to tell anyone, but he entered it in some short-story competition at a bookstore in Seattle. He swears he can get it back. And if Carrie wins, she gets a gift certificate worth a hundred bucks. What should we do?

1:53 P.M. Sky passes a note back to Alex:

Whatever you do, do not tell Carrie. You heard what she said yesterday. She'll kill Jordan if she finds out. (Not that I would mind.) The best thing to do is just wait and see what happens. And if she talks any more about some conspiracy involving The Amys, we should just play along. Besides, it would be really cool if she won, right?

3:15 P.M. By the time Carrie boards the bus to go home, she is almost certain that The Amys are responsible. Alex, Sky, Jordan, and Sam listen with glazed expressions as she outlines her theory. Yesterday when she got on the bus, Mel was standing in the aisle, blocking her path. Carrie's back was turned to Amy, who was sitting in the front seat. Amy had just enough time to unzip the front pocket of her book bag and swipe the story. So now they need to plot revenge, right? Right?

Five

"Hello?" Carrie called as she walked through the front door. "Mom?"

There was no answer. Her voice echoed off the bare white walls and peach-and-white checkered marble floor of the front hallway.

"Hello?" she called again.

But the house was empty. Well, *that* was a relief. She needed relief. Today may very well have been one of the worst days of her thirteen-year-old life.

Even her best friends were acting strange. Carrie couldn't understand it. Why didn't they want to get The Amys back for taking her story? Why didn't they even want to *talk* about it? Under circumstances like these, all five of them should have been busy plotting the most wicked, masterful, horrific sort of revenge imaginable. But it seemed as if they didn't even care all that much that Carrie's story had been stolen in the *first* place.

It wasn't fair.

If The Amys had stolen Alex's skateboard, *she* would have gone ballistic. Or what about Jordan? He would have thrown a fit if The Amys had stolen his sketch pad.

Oh, well. There was no point obsessing about it. If they wanted to let her fight this battle alone, then that's what she would have to do. At least she had her typewriter. Her typewriter never let her down. The worn keys would provide all the comfort, friendship, and support she needed right now. In fact, she would just rewrite her story from start to finish—and make it even *better*. The Amys could *have* her story. . . .

"Stupid, lousy Amys," she muttered.

On her way to the stairs, she noticed that the message light on the answering machine in the living room was blinking. She marched into the living room and punched the play button.

The tinny, computerized phone voice announced: "Message One . . . Received . . . Wednesday, two-thirty-two P.M."

"Hi! This is a message for Carrie Mersel."

Carrie frowned. It wasn't her mom. It was some bubbly woman she'd never heard before.

"It's Peggy Wallace from the Second Avenue branch of the Cheshire Cat Bookstore. Congratulations! After careful consideration, our two judges have selected your story, "The Three Girls Who Lived on the Hill," as the winner in our fiction contest. As you know, you will receive a gift certificate . . ."

Carrie's eyes bulged. Her book bag slipped from her shoulder and fell to the carpet with a loud *thud*. But she hardly noticed. Her whole body was frozen stiff. The seconds seemed to crawl by in slow motion as the message went on and on.

". . . and congratulations again! Bye!"

What the . . .

In a flash, she jabbed her finger at the play button on the machine again.

"Hi! This is a message for Carrie Mersel . . ."

Carrie held her breath and leaned close to the speaker. Well, one thing was for sure: This was obviously some sort of prank. She couldn't place the voice—but that didn't mean anything. The woman could have been one of Amy Anderson's older sisters. She could have been Amy

Anderson's *mom*, for all Carrie knew.

". . . you will receive a gift certificate of one hundred dollars off a purchase at any Cheshire Cat Bookstore. And, of course, we would love to have you read your story at our store this Sunday at one P.M. We'll be serving cider and a light snack. So tell all your friends! Please call me back at . . ."

Carrie snatched a notebook and pen out of her book bag and wrote down the number. Knowing The Amys, the number probably belonged to some local chat line that cost three-ninety-nine a minute. Of course, there was an easy way to find out if the number *didn't* belong to the Cheshire Cat Bookstore. She could check the Seattle white pages.

". . . and congratulations again! Bye!" The machine beeped and went off.

Carrie laughed once. She had to admit, The Amys had pulled off a good one. Whoever that woman was, she sounded pretty genuine.

"Cheshire Cat Bookstore . . . ," Carrie murmured. She pulled the phone book out of the drawer in the telephone table and squinted at the small print as she flipped through the pages.

41

There.

Her finger ran down the list of Cheshire Cat Bookstore numbers until it reached the Second Avenue branch. Then her eyes flashed back to the number she had written down.

The numbers were the same.

Carrie chewed her lip. Well, that didn't mean anything, either. Nothing would be more humiliating than calling up a bookstore to accept some prize that didn't exist, right?

She stared at the phone for a moment. Should she call? If she did, she would be falling right into The Amys' trap. Then again, she already knew what to expect. Maybe it was best to call and just get the whole thing over with. Then her mind would be clear. Once her mind was clear, she could get down to the business of plotting a counterstrike.

She grabbed the phone and quickly dialed the number. After one ring, someone picked up.

"Cheshire Cat Bookstore, Second Avenue branch," a woman answered.

"Uh . . . yes, hi." Carrie cleared her throat. "I'm, uh, calling for Peggy Wallace."

"This is Peggy Wallace," the woman replied. "Who's this?"

Carrie didn't answer right away.

For some reason, she had suddenly started to feel strangely queasy. Her lips and tongue were dry.

"I'm Carrie Mersel," she croaked after a moment.

"Carrie!" the woman cried. Her voice *was* the same as the voice on the message. "I'm so glad to hear from you. We all just *loved* your piece. And when I found out that you were only in the eighth grade, I was so impressed—"

"W-W-wait," Carrie stuttered. Her heart was bouncing violently in her chest. "How did you *get* my . . . uh, piece?"

"Your friend dropped it off last night," the woman said, sounding a little confused. "Didn't you—"

Carrie immediately slammed the phone down on the hook.

Her entire body was trembling.

Then she blinked.

Jeez, she said to herself. *Why did I just hang up on that woman?*

She reached for the phone again, then

hesitated, then reached again—and finally let her hand drop. A long, quivering breath escaped her lips. Okay, before she did anything else, she clearly just needed to *sit*.

Her knees were wobbling like two little bowls of Jell-O. Still, she managed to slide herself onto the lone peach couch in the sprawling, barren room.

Had she really won some kind of prize?

Her instincts told her that it was impossible. But The Amys couldn't have planted someone at a bookstore in Seattle to intercept her call. They weren't *that* good. So what was going on here? Who on earth had stolen her story, brought it all the way to the Cheshire Cat Bookstore in Seattle, and entered it in some fiction contest?

Alex.

Of course. It *had* to have been Alex.

Alex was the one who had made such a big deal of trying to get Carrie to show the story to someone in the first place. And Alex was the one who had been making potato salad in the kitchen yesterday—*alone*, with Carrie's book bag. And now that Carrie thought about it, Alex was *also* the one who was the least psyched to pull any kind of prank on The Amys.

That's because she knew The Amys were innocent.

It all made sense now.

A crazy jumble of emotions began to swirl through her mind. She literally felt as if her brain was being wrenched in a dozen different directions. Part of her was kind of mad. *Really* mad, in a way. Alex had gone behind her back when she had specifically said she would kill anyone who tried to do anything with her story. She'd been joking, of course—but she'd made it clear that she hadn't wanted to share her story with *anyone*. Her stories were for her friends and herself. That was it.

Another part of her was a little hurt, too. Alex had lied to her this whole time, even though Carrie had been miserable.

But the last part of her, a part that was buried beneath everything else, was . . . well, *what?* Thrilled? Not exactly. Excited? Sort of. Maybe just baffled—and definitely the tiniest bit happy, too.

Somebody had actually been *impressed* with something she wrote.

And for the briefest instant, she had a weird little daydream. She saw herself standing with a big trophy in front of a huge crowd of people.

"Thank you, thank you. I'd just like to say that I never thought I'd be the youngest writer ever to win the Nobel prize. And let me just offer a bit of advice to those other young writers out there. Don't write for glory and adulation and fame. Those things are all great, of course. But the only way you're going to get where I've gotten is by . . ."

Okay, enough of that.

The reality of the situation was that there was no *way* she would get up and read her story in front of a bunch of strangers at a Seattle bookstore. In fact, she wouldn't even bother calling Peggy Wallace back. The woman probably thought she was insane, anyway. Nope—there was only one call Carrie had to make.

And that was to the person who had gotten her into this whole mess in the first place.

Six

Alex was far too wound up to sit still. She kept pacing back and forth, gathering up piles of dirty laundry, putting them on her chair or bed, then picking them up and throwing them on the floor again. One of these days, she was going to straighten herself out cleaningwise. She was a total slob—and she knew it. But no matter what she did, her room never seemed to get any less messy.

Maybe she should just get out of here. She had to do *something* to take her mind off Carrie and her missing story and Jordan's cover-up. Maybe she should skateboard over to Sam's place and see if he wanted to work on some new tricks.

"Alex?" her father called from downstairs. "Is everything all right up there?"

"Uh . . . yeah," she said uncertainly. "Why?"

"Well, I gotta tell you—all the stomping is making me a little jumpy," he replied.

Oops. Sometimes it was easy to forget that this house was also her father's office. In fact, it was pretty easy to forget that he was even *there* a lot of the time.

"Sorry," she called back. She bounded down the stairs and grabbed her skateboard out of the front hall closet.

"I'm going over to Sam's," she announced. "I'll be back before six."

"Bye," he called.

She was halfway out the door when the phone rang.

"Got it!" she yelled, dropping the skateboard and dashing back inside to the kitchen.

Sam could wait. Because hopefully the person calling was Jordan. Hopefully Jordan was calling to tell her that he had confessed what he had done, and that Carrie had forgiven him, and that she had won the prize, and that everything was great. . . .

"Hello?" Alex asked breathlessly.

"Hi, Alex!"

Alex blinked. It wasn't Jordan. It was

48

Carrie. A very happy-sounding Carrie. An almost weirdly cheerful Carrie . . .

"Alex?" Carrie asked in the silence. "Are you there?"

"Uh, yeah . . . um, sorry," Alex said. She couldn't figure out what was going on— unless Jordan had already talked to her. Was it possible that he had somehow returned the story? Or even better, had Carrie won the contest?

"So . . . what's up?" Alex asked.

"Oh, nothing," Carrie said breezily. "What's up with you?"

Alex hesitated. "Not much," she replied. There was a silence.

"It's a nice day," Carrie said after a moment.

"Uh . . . yup," Alex answered cautiously. "Sure is."

"How come you're not outside?" Carrie asked. "Are you reading?"

Alex's eyes narrowed. *Reading?* She couldn't put her finger on it, but there was something strange about that question. It sounded . . . well, *formal* or something. "No," she said. "Why?"

"Well, I figured since you were at a

bookstore, you might have picked up a good book."

"Bookstore?" Alex asked confusedly. "Uh . . . what do you mean?"

"You didn't buy anything when you dropped off my story?" Carrie asked as casually as ever.

Uh-oh. "Carrie, I—"

"Alex, I *know* you gave my story to the Cheshire Cat Bookstore in Seattle," Carrie interrupted. The funny thing was, she didn't even sound mad. She just sounded extremely sure of herself. "See, there was this message on my machine when I got home. Apparently, *somebody* entered my story in a fiction competition, even though I stated very clearly that the penalty for something like that would be death."

Alex bit her lip. So, Carrie *had* found out the truth—and not from Jordan. No, Carrie thought *she* was responsible. But still, Alex couldn't help but wonder if the message from the bookstore meant that Carrie won. And *that* was the important thing.

"What did the message say?" Alex asked.

There was another pause.

"Carrie?" Alex prodded.

"Well, I won," Carrie murmured.

"Carrie, that's awesome!" Alex exclaimed excitedly. "Congratulations!"

"Thanks," Carrie mumbled. "I still don't really believe it, but . . ."

"What are you *talking* about?" Alex laughed. "I *knew* people would love your stuff! I just knew it. See, didn't I tell you?"

"Yeah, but that's not the point, Alex," Carrie said quietly. She didn't sound quite as cheerful as she had before. "The point is that you stole my story and gave it to somebody when I told you not to. And then you *lied* about it."

Alex didn't say anything for a moment. *Hmm.* In a way, Carrie was right. Alex had known the truth all day, and she still hadn't told Carrie. That *was* sort of lying.

"*Why* did you do it?" Carrie asked. "I mean . . . why?"

All at once, Alex knew she had to make a choice. Either she could come clean and tell Carrie that Jordan was the one who had submitted the story—or she could take the blame herself.

She fidgeted absently with the bill of her Supersonics cap. She *could* just tell Carrie the

51

whole truth right now. But if she did, she would have to rat on Jordan. And Jordan had only submitted Carrie's story because he figured he was doing something nice for her. Besides, Alex Wagner did *not* rat on people, no matter what the circumstances were. Taking the blame was still a lot better than being a tattletale.

No, if Carrie was going to hear the truth, she would have to hear it from Jordan himself.

"Well?" Carrie asked.

"Uh . . . sorry," Alex said finally.

Carrie sighed. "That still doesn't answer my question, Alex," she said.

"Well, let me ask *you* something," Alex said. "Aren't you psyched? I mean, you're going to be reading your story in front of—"

"No way, Jose," Carrie stated, cutting Alex off in midsentence. "I'm not reading my story in front of *anyone*."

Alex shook her head. "But why not? Don't you—"

"Because I don't *want* to," Carrie said simply. "And it's *my* decision to make."

There was no way Alex could argue with that.

"You know, it's funny," Carrie said after a moment.

"What's funny?" Alex asked.

"That you don't learn. After you dragged me to Amy Anderson's last week and caused a whole huge fight, you *still* went and did something like this."

Alex swallowed. Maybe taking the blame *hadn't* been such a good idea. "I told you, I'm sorry," she said. "I didn't know—"

"I *know* you're sorry." Carrie let out a deep breath. "Look, just forget it, all right? I'll see you tomorrow."

Alex frowned. "Wait, you're not mad, are you?"

"Of *course* I'm mad!" Carrie cried. "I'm supposed to read my story in front of a bunch of perfect strangers! Wouldn't *you* be mad if one of *your* friends got you into a mess like that?"

Alex thought about that for a second. Would *she* be mad if she had won some prize? Probably not. "No, I don't think so—"

"Good-bye, Alex," Carrie groaned.

"Wait—"

But before Alex could get another word in, the line clicked and went dead.

<u>Alex Wagner</u> 's Book <u>of</u> <u>Deep</u> <u>Thoughts</u>

<u>Entry</u> 6

Well I said that this was going to be a very, very interesting week, didn't I?

<u>Interesting</u> is one of my favorite words. It can mean almost anything. On one hand, it might mean something that really grabs your attention, like: "Hey, that motori<u>zed</u> skateboard is really interesting." On the other hand, it can describe something that is totally lame, like: "Hey, that pink dress you're wearing is really interesting."

Right now, I'm pretty much in an "interesting" position. Either I keep lying, or I rat on Jordan. And after I lied to Carrie and Sky about Amy Anderson inviting all <u>three</u> of us to her house last week, I swore I'd never lie again. I never thought one tiny little lie could cause so much trouble. But it did. That one little lie caused the worst fight Carrie and I have ever had. Yep, lying to your friends is definitely one of the worst things you can do. It's almost as bad as . . . well, ratting on one of them.

If I do rat on Jordan (not that I would), I would essentially be admitting to Carrie that I lied just now on the phone. And lying was why she got so mad at me to begin with. But I wasn't lying before. Or I was only partially lying.

I guess Carrie was right. It is kind of funny that I didn't learn anything from our fight. I still ended up making a huge mistake. And you want to know what's really funny? I'm not even sure what kind of mistake it was.

Now that's funny.

Come to think of it, funny is another one of those words like interesting. It can mean pretty much anything.

In my case it means: not funny at all.

Seven

Uh-oh.

The moment Sky climbed on board the bus the next morning, she knew that something had happened. Something *bad*.

For one thing, Alex wasn't wearing her green Supersonics cap—the one she had stolen from Matt. She *always* wore that hat. Especially when it rained.

There was something else, too. Sky noticed it when she was about halfway down the mud-splattered aisle. Carrie and Alex were sitting *way* too far apart.

It was totally bizarre. Carrie was sitting closer to Jordan than she was to Alex. Sky's usual place had disappeared. Instead of one big empty space, there were now two little empty spaces on each side of Carrie. Sky wouldn't fit in either of them. She was skinny, but she wasn't *that* skinny.

"What's going on here?" she asked. "How come there's no room for me anymore?"

Nobody answered. Raindrops pelted the windows. It was a sour, wet, gray morning—and everyone's mood obviously matched.

"Well?" she prodded.

Carrie cast a sidelong glance at Alex.

Oh no, Sky groaned silently. Were Carrie and Alex in another fight? She didn't know if she could deal with *that* again. Their last fight had almost given her a nervous breakdown. Anyway, why would they be mad at each other? If anyone should have been in a fight, it should have been Carrie and Jordan—not Carrie and Alex. *He* was the one who had stolen Carrie's story.

Her eyes shifted to Jordan. Yes, something weird was definitely going on here. Jordan was staring forlornly at his lap. He actually looked a little pale. "All right," she breathed. "What happened?"

"You gotta sit down, Sky," Brick, the bus driver, called before anyone could answer. "Sorry, but that's the rule."

"Yeah," Amy Anderson chimed in from the front seat. "We're all getting tired of looking at your rear end, anyway."

A few kids laughed.

Sky didn't even bother to turn around. She didn't have the energy to get involved with The Amys right now. But she *did* want to sit down.

"Come on, *move*, you guys," she pleaded.

Finally, Carrie slid aside to make room for her. But instead of sliding to her right, as usual, she slid to her left—next to Jordan.

Sky reluctantly lowered herself between Carrie and Alex.

Sitting in this spot felt so . . . *off*. They'd never sat this way before. Ever.

"Will somebody *please* tell me what's going on?" she asked.

"You honestly don't know?" Carrie said dubiously.

Sky shook her head.

"You have no idea that Alex stole my story and gave it to some bookstore behind my back?" Carrie asked.

Sky's jaw dropped. *"Alex?"* she cried. She leaned forward and shot a bewildered look at Jordan. "You think *Alex* was the one who did it? Why?"

Carrie's hazel eyes narrowed. "Why

shouldn't I?" she asked slowly. "Is there something I don't know?"

"Well, yeah," Sky said. She kept staring at Jordan. But he didn't seem to see her. He was hunched forward in the seat, staring at his sneakers.

"You don't have to say anything if you don't want to, Jordan," Alex said. "I'll understand."

All right, now Sky was *totally* confused. This wasn't making any sense. Why did Carrie think Alex had stolen her story? Why wasn't Jordan saying anything? Carrie was clearly as confused as she was. Her head kept rapidly turning between Jordan and Alex.

"Jordan?" Sky asked.

Finally, Jordan leaned back in his seat and sighed. He brushed a few rain-soaked strands of blond hair out of his eyes. "Look, Carrie, I was the one who took your story and entered it in the contest, okay?"

Carrie's gray eyes looked as if they were about to pop out of her head. *"What?"*

Jordan shrugged. "I'm sorry. I didn't know it was going to turn out to be such a big deal."

"And?" Sky prompted.

Jordan frowned. "What do you mean, 'and'?"

"*And* Alex had nothing to do with it," Sky finished. Carrie's head swiveled around. "Wait a second. How do *you* know? I thought you said you had no idea what was going on!"

Sky shrugged. "Alex told me."

Alex started shaking her head. "Sky, I told you not to tell—"

"What?" Sky asked defensively. "She already knows—"

"Alex, why did you tell Sky?" Jordan groaned. "You swore you wouldn't tell anyone."

"Oh, come on, Jordan," Sam mumbled. "*You* told me."

Sky winced. *Uh-oh.* This probably wasn't the best conversation to be having in front of Carrie right now. . . .

Carrie sat up straight.

"Okay, so let me get this straight," she said very carefully. "Jordan was the one who stole my story. Not Alex. And everyone knows except *me*. Now why is that?" Her voice rose. "Why does everybody know what happened to *my* story except me?"

Sky didn't know how to respond to that

question. Apparently nobody else did, either. The tense silence lasted until the bus turned onto the semicircular drive in front of the school building and screeched to a halt next to the front doors.

Carrie was the first one to get up. She turned to face them.

"I don't know what you guys were thinking," she said. "But if one of *you* ever wants to . . . wants to . . ." She threw her hands up. "Oh, just forget it!" She whirled and marched down the aisle.

For a long time, nobody moved.

"So," Jordan finally said with a big fake smile. "You think Carrie is still gonna want to split the prize money with me?"

Eight

Alex was a wreck. There was no way she could possibly concentrate on *anything* until she talked to Carrie. But Carrie was obviously trying to avoid the four of them. She hadn't been in any of her usual spots all morning: not in the girls' bathroom, not in the hall outside her English class—not even near her locker.

Finally, right before lunch, Alex caught a glimpse of a familiar black sweater through a swarm of kids in the hall by the boys' lockers. Carrie was standing a few feet from the big double doors that led to the cafeteria. In fact, she was standing right near Jordan's locker.

Alex picked up her pace. That wasn't a good sign.

"Carrie!" she shouted, jostling through the crowd to catch up with her. "Hey!"

Carrie didn't look particularly overjoyed

to see her—but at least she didn't make any effort to move. "What's up?" she muttered as Alex approached.

"I'm so glad I found you." Alex took a deep breath. "I want to explain exactly what happened."

Carrie pursed her lips. "I *know* exactly what happened. I was on the bus, too, remember?"

"Look, Jordan didn't know you'd be so upset," Alex explained. "How could he have known? He wasn't there on Monday. He thought he was doing you a favor—"

"What I want to know is how he got a hold of it in the first place," Carrie interrupted. "How did he know to look in my knapsack?"

Alex lowered her eyes. "Well, I told him it was in there," she admitted sheepishly. "But I had no idea he would *take* it with him when he left my house. Anyway, he didn't know that it was your only copy."

Carrie just shook her head. "That *still* doesn't change the fact that all of you knew what was going on this whole time. And you still didn't tell me."

"I only found out yesterday!" Alex cried.

Carrie laughed. "Yeah—*before* I called. You could have told me exactly what happened.

63

But instead you didn't tell me *anything*. You even made it seem like *you* were the one who did it." She paused, wrinkling her brow. "Why did you do that, anyway? You must have known I'd freak out on you."

"Exactly," Alex stated, looking her straight in the eye. "I knew you'd freak out on me."

Carrie blinked. "Uh . . . you're gonna have to help me out here, Alex. I'm not following you."

Alex opened her mouth, but then she hesitated. How could she possibly say what she wanted to say without totally offending Carrie? *"I knew you'd freak, because that's what you always do."* No, that wouldn't work. Somehow she needed to show Carrie—*gently*, of course—that Carrie occasionally let her anger get the best of her. Like now, for instance.

"See, I didn't want to tell on Jordan," Alex began. She waited until everyone else in the hall had disappeared through the cafeteria doors. This was going to be really, really difficult. She unconsciously reached for the bill of her Supersonics cap. *Whoops.* It wasn't there. Her hand dropped clumsily to her side. She struggled to keep her train of thought.

A brief, forgiving smile passed over Carrie's lips. Alex had to smile, too. It was almost as if Carrie was telling her: "Alex, just go ahead and say whatever you want, you big dork."

"Listen, I know you're morally opposed to telling on people," Carrie said casually, breaking the silence. "And that's generally a very cool and noble thing. *Generally.*"

Alex sighed. "But that's not the only reason I took the blame for him," she said. "Look, promise you won't get mad if I say something?"

Carrie cocked an eyebrow. "That's kind of like saying, 'Promise you won't laugh,' right? And the last time you said *that* to me, I ended up laughing so hard I almost stopped breathing."

"Well, let me start by asking you something," Alex said. "Why are you hanging around Jordan's locker right now?"

"Why do you think?" Carrie asked. She glanced in either direction down the long empty hall. "But I guess he had enough sense to avoid me."

"*That's* what I'm talking about," Alex stated. "You were going to . . . well, you were going to yell at him or something.

But why? He wouldn't have handed your story over to the bookstore if he thought he was doing something wrong, right?"

"I *know*," Carrie said. Her voice hardened. "But that *still* doesn't change the fact that he took my story without asking me."

"But he didn't know that was wrong, either!" Alex cried. "Carrie, sometimes you can be kind of hard on people, you know that? And a lot of times, they don't even *know* they've done a bad thing. That's why I didn't want to tell you it was Jordan."

Carrie didn't answer for a few seconds. "Now I see why you wanted to make me promise not to get mad," she mumbled.

Alex sighed again. "Anyway, the whole point of all this stuff really has nothing to *do* with Jordan. The whole point is that you won a prize for something you wrote. And that's amazing." Her voice softened. "You should be really, really psyched."

Carrie looked at the floor. "I *am* psyched," she said quietly.

"So why are you mad at Jordan?" Alex asked, raising her hands.

The faint beginnings of a grin began to

appear at the corners of Carrie's mouth. "Well, if it makes you feel any better, I probably won't be able to stay mad at Jordan for much longer," she said, shifting on her feet.

Alex laughed. "That's good—but you know what would make *all* of us feel better? If you took the prize and went through with the reading."

Carrie looked up at her. "Alex, that's *not* going to happen."

"Why not?"

Carrie's gaze fell to the floor again. "It's just . . . I don't know," she said quietly. "I don't want to make a jerk of myself. What if everyone hates it?"

"How can they possibly hate it?" Alex cried in disbelief. "It *won*, remember?"

Carrie shook her head. "I'm not talking about the people who chose the story. I'm talking about the people who happen to wander in off the street. I'm talking about the ones who see some dorky thirteen-year-old girl reading her lame story and then decide to start throwing rotten apple cores at her."

Alex's eyes widened. She couldn't believe what she was hearing. Was this really Carrie Mersel talking? There couldn't have been a more un-Carrie-ish thing to say than to describe herself as "dorky." Carrie was the Queen of Confidence, the Princess of Put-downs. . . .

"What?" Carrie asked.

Alex shook her head. "Man, Jordan was right: You *are* paranoid. You won. Don't you get it? People *want* to hear your story."

Carrie snorted.

Alex smiled. "Well, will you at least *think* about it?" she pleaded. "Can you do that?"

"Yes, Alex, I can do that," Carrie sighed. "Now can we please eat? We're gonna miss lunch if we keep arguing."

"Well . . . okay."

Alex figured she'd leave it at that for now. At least it was a start, right?

Nine

"Hi, honey, I'm home!" Mrs. Mersel sang out cheerfully from downstairs. "How was your day, dear?"

"Fine," Carrie answered from her room. At least, she *thought* she was fine. She wasn't quite sure. She'd been sprawled across her bed for the past two hours, staring out the window at the rain and trying to figure out whether or not to take Alex's advice. Amazingly enough, there was this part of her that really *did* want to read. In fact, she was actually starting to get kind of psyched.

There was a light knock on her door.

"Come in," Carrie called.

Mrs. Mersel strolled right in and immediately turned the light on. Carrie squinted at the sudden brightness.

"It's so *dark* in here," Mrs. Mersel murmured. She was holding some kind of catalog. She placed it next to the antique typewriter on Carrie's rickety oak desk, then smoothed some imaginary wrinkles from her pleated suit and sat in the desk chair.

"What's that?" Carrie asked, sitting up straight and rubbing her eyes.

"I wanted you to help me pick out a laptop computer," she said, patting the catalog with a big smile. The desk wobbled slightly under her hand.

Carrie shook her head, smirking. How many times did they have to have this *same* conversation? "Mom, I told you, my typewriter—"

"And while we're at it, we ought to get you a new desk, too," Mrs. Mersel put in. "I think you've just about outgrown this one, wouldn't you say? It's about to fall apart."

Oh, brother, Carrie said to herself. Why did her mom always have to mention the desk? She knew perfectly well how much it meant to her. But things like old-fashioned charm and sentimental value didn't mean much to her mom. If it wasn't brand-spanking new, it wasn't worth having around.

"It's *not* about to fall apart, Mom," she said after a moment. "It's always been a little unsteady like that."

70

"Are you telling me in all honesty that you'd prefer to work at an unsteady desk?" her mom asked, raising her perfectly shaped blond eyebrows.

"Yup," Carrie said. Her lips started to curl into a grin. It was time to change the subject. And she knew the perfect way to convince her mom that she was doing just fine with a battered old desk and typewriter. "I need it for inspiration," she said.

Mrs. Mersel laughed. "What *sort* of inspiration, dear?"

"Inspiration for my prizewinning stories," Carrie said, lamely trying to mask the excitement in her voice.

Her mom just looked at her. "Prize-winning stories?"

Carrie nodded—and then all at once, the words started tumbling out of her mouth. "Well, you know that story I thought I lost? See, Jordan entered it in a fiction contest at this bookstore in Seattle. I didn't even know what happened until I got home yesterday. And guess what? I won! I get a hundred-dollar certificate. I also have to give a reading of the story at the bookstore this Sunday." She was beaming now. "Isn't that crazy?"

71

Mrs. Mersel nodded. But her expression hadn't changed. "That's very nice, dear," she stated.

Carrie blinked. "Nice?" she repeated.

Her mom nodded again. The ever-present smile remained stuck to her face, as if it had been painted on. "Well, dear, it's just that we know that you do fine in English class," she said. "But there's no way you can do this reading on Sunday. After all, the first math test of the year is on Monday."

Carrie's own smile abruptly vanished. "What does *that* have to do with anything?" she asked uncomprehendingly.

"It has to do with *priorities*, honey," Mrs. Mersel said. "Your father and I are concerned you don't have your priorities straight."

"Dad?" she asked. What did *he* care? He was never even *home.* And when he was, he was either on the computer or on the phone or in front of the TV.

"Look, Carrie, the point is that your father and I both know that you've always had difficulty with math," her mother went on. "And you're in the eighth grade now. You're going to be in high school next year. You need to focus on what's important. You need to study, dear. It's that simple. You can read one of your stories whenever you like, but . . ."

Carrie found she couldn't even listen. At first, she hadn't even taken her mom seriously. But now all her happiness, all her enthusiasm, all her pride—*everything* she had experienced today—swiftly fizzled into nothingness. Her mom hadn't even offered her a "Congratulations," or a "By the way—I'm proud of you." Nope. Nothing. All she could do was give a lecture about some dinky little geometry quiz.

". . . so it's time that you get—"

"Mom, I'm going to do *fine* on the stupid test!" Carrie yelled.

Her mother jumped slightly. "Carrie, *please*," she whispered. "There's no need to raise your voice."

Carrie looked her in the eye. "Mom—I *won* a contest for my writing," she said in a quavering voice. "Does that mean anything to you?"

Mrs. Mersel nodded. "Well, of course, dear," she said briskly. "But this is important."

"Important?" Carrie demanded. She tried to swallow, but much to her surprise, a lump had formed in her throat. She was shaking. This was crazy. Her mom wasn't even on the same *wavelength*.

"I really don't understand why you're getting so upset," Mrs. Mersel murmured. "All I'm saying is that you need to prioritize a little. Writing stories is fine—as long as you have a handle on your studies."

"A handle on my studies," Carrie repeated in a strained voice. Her eyes were starting to get teary. She sniffed. Her nose was running. She didn't even know *why* she was getting so worked up. Her mom was just doing the same thing she always did.

"Carrie, what's wrong?" her mom asked.

"Nothing," she choked out. She lay back down on the bed and curled up into a little ball, squeezing her eyes shut. "I'm sorry. I'm not . . . I'm not in the mood to talk right now."

The room was quiet for a few moments. "All right," Mrs. Mersel said with a sigh. "But we *will* talk about this later. We have to talk about it sometime."

The door closed behind her.

Carrie rubbed her eyes. Talk about *what* later? There was nothing to talk about.

Well, one thing was certain. She was *not* going to cry. No, she was going to do something about her life. She was going to show her mom, her dad—and everyone else, for that matter—that she *did* have her priorities straight.

Without hesitating, she opened her eyes and reached for the phone on the nightstand by her bed, then dialed the number for the Cheshire Cat Bookstore.

"Cheshire Cat Bookstore, Second Avenue branch," a woman answered.

Carrie was pretty sure she recognized the woman's voice. "Uh . . . is this Peggy Wallace?" she asked. Her voice was a little hoarse.

"Yes," she replied. "Who's this?"

Carrie managed a smile. "This is Carrie Mersel again," she said. "I, uh, think we got cut off yesterday."

"Carrie! I'm glad to hear from you again."

Carrie swallowed. "I, uh, just want to say that I'm really honored you chose my story. I'd love to do the reading on Sunday," she said, sniffing again.

"Terrific," the woman answered. "I'm so pleased."

"Uh . . . so is there anything I need to do?" Carrie asked hesitantly.

She laughed. "No, no, Carrie. We'll handle everything. Just be here no later than twelve forty-five on Sunday, all right? Oh—and be sure to tell all your friends."

"I will," Carrie said. She was very sure she would do that. She was going to tell everyone she knew—*except* her mother. And The Amys, of course.

"So we'll see you then?" the woman asked.

"Right," Carrie said. "Thanks again. Bye."

"Good-bye! And thank *you!*"

Carrie placed the phone down on the hook.

Well, *that* had been easy. She waited for the rush of triumph.

So where was it?

She thought she would feel *something*. She thought she would at least feel like she had won a minor little victory over her mother. But she didn't. Instead, she just felt vaguely nauseated. In fact, there was only one thought running through her mind.

What did I just get myself into?

Ten

Jordan was nervous. And he was hardly ever nervous before lunch. In fact, lunch was the one time of day when Jordan was pretty sure he could avoid getting in trouble. But judging from the way Carrie had been acting all morning, he figured his luck was about to change. It wasn't that she was *angry* . . . No, it was more that she was silent. And a little sad, as well. She'd hardly said a word on the bus this morning. In fact, it seemed as if she were purposely avoiding the subject of the stolen story altogether.

But sooner or later, she was going to let him have it. He was sure of it.

And now he could see that Carrie was already at the table. Everybody else was, too. Jordan set down his tray, then slumped into his chair.

"I've been waiting for you," Carrie said.

Here we go, Jordan thought. He glanced up, holding his breath.

"I wanted to tell everybody at the same time," she went on. A half smile broke on her face. "I'm going to do the reading."

"What?" Jordan gasped. That was about the *last* thing he expected to hear.

Sky was already clapping her hands excitedly. "Carrie, that's totally awesome!" she exclaimed. "What made you change your mind?"

Carrie shrugged. "A couple of things," she said dryly. "But mostly it was my mom. She told me that I couldn't do the reading because I needed to study for a math test. That clinched it."

Jordan shook his head, but he was laughing. Only Carrie would agree to do something she dreaded *specifically* because her mom told her not to.

"Look, Carrie, I'm really sorry about the whole thing," he began. "I didn't mean—"

"Don't worry about it," she interrupted gently. She waved one of her hands. "Seriously. I mean, next time you pull something like that, you *will* end up at the bottom of Puget Sound wearing a pair of concrete shoes." She smiled at him. "But right now you're off the hook."

Jordan smirked. "Thanks."

"So, anyway, it would be cool if you guys could come," she said hesitantly. She lowered her eyes. "I mean, if you're not doing anything . . ."

"Not *doing* anything?" Jordan cried. "What are you, kidding? We wouldn't miss this for the world. We're all gonna be in the front row."

"Cheering at the top of our lungs," Alex added.

"We're gonna be your biggest fans," Sky said.

Jordan nodded eagerly. "I'm gonna video the whole thing," he said. "And listen, if you want to practice or anything beforehand, you can just come over to my house. Seriously. I can be like your voice coach—"

Eeerk!

There was a deafening screech.

Everybody at the table flinched. At first Jordan didn't even know what the noise was. But then he saw Ms. Lloyd standing in front of the old and seldom-used microphone near the kitchen.

"Sorry about the feedback," Miss Lloyd said with a nervous little chuckle.

Her normally mousy voice boomed across the cafeteria. She sounded like Darth Vader or something. It was kind of frightening.

"Anyway, I have an announcement to make," she said.

The lunchroom grew quiet.

"Maybe she's getting married," Carrie hissed.

"Eww!" Sky whispered.

Miss Lloyd smiled broadly. "Last night I happened to be at a bookstore in Seattle—the Cheshire Cat."

Cheshire Cat? Jordan nearly fell out of his chair. He shot a look at Carrie. She wasn't smiling anymore. In fact, she looked a little greenish.

"And as I was walking out the door, I noticed a poster with a familiar name," Ms. Lloyd continued. Her own smile widened.

"To make a long story short, it turns out that our very own Carrie Mersel has been leading a double life as a famous writer. This Sunday at one, Carrie will be reading her short story, *The Three Girls Who Lived on the Hill*, at the Cheshire Cat. The story took first prize at a fiction contest. The contest was only supposed to be open to high school students, I might add. So I felt the need to say congratulations. It's very impressive. We're all quite proud of you."

She started clapping.

The cafeteria was instantly filled with the thunderous sound of applause.

Jordan couldn't believe it. Now the whole *school* knew. A moment later, he was pounding his hands together along with the rest of them. Everyone at the table was smiling—except Carrie, of course, whose face had gone from green to bright red in about three seconds. She buried her face in her hands.

Amy Anderson suddenly leapt out of her chair. "I think it's just great that one of our schoolmates is being recognized for her talents!" she shouted excitedly.

Oh, please, Jordan thought. Leave it to Amy to try to attract attention to herself at a moment like this. She sounded like a game show host.

"So I think we owe it to ourselves as a school to go out and support her, right?" she cried. "I know *I* will! Huh? What do you say . . . ?"

Jordan frowned. He wanted to stick a sock down her throat—anything to shut her up. But as she went on, he noticed something. Aimee Stewart wasn't sitting at the table with Amy anymore. And Mel Eng was staring right at Carrie. . . .

Oh no.

Out of the corner of his eye, he saw someone coming up behind them. *Fast.*

He whirled around.

Aimee was right there. Jordan froze. She was pointing a huge water gun at Carrie. Before Jordan even had time to open his mouth, Aimee was pulling the trigger. He watched in numb horror as a thick, sloppy spray of water soaked the back of Carrie's black skirt.

"Yow!" Carrie shrieked, leaping out of her chair.

"What's going on?" Ms. Lloyd demanded into the microphone.

There was a moment of confusion as everyone glanced around the cafeteria. Aimee turned and bolted out the double doors.

Jordan tried to get up to chase her, to do *something*—but his legs seemed to have turned to putty.

"Gross!" Amy Anderson cried, abruptly ending her little speech. "Carrie wet her pants!"

Then everyone turned at once.

No, Jordan thought desperately. *No, no, no . . .*

But it was too late.

Now every other seventh- and eighth-grader at Robert Lowell was staring at Carrie, too. More specifically, they were staring at her sopping wet rear end.

Jordan felt the color draining from her cheeks. *This can't be happening.*

There were a few scattered chuckles.

Amy shook her head disappointedly. "Carrie, we know you're excited, but still . . . did you have to pee in your pants?"

"Amy!" Ms. Lloyd's voice thundered across the cafeteria. "Enough!"

The entire lunchroom started cracking up.

And at that moment, Carrie simply fled. She disappeared through the same double doors where Aimee had vanished only moments ago.

Only then did Jordan realize what had happened—and *why*.

"Now we're even," Amy hissed.

Alex Wagner's Book of Deep Thoughts

Entry 7

If Amy actually thinks she got even with us after that stupid little water gun stunt today at school, she's a bigger loser than I thought.

Not that I—or we, for that matter—have any intention of letting it slide. No way. We're going to get her back. And whatever we do, it's going to make the last prank we pulled seem like we were sending a Hallmark card or something.

But right now, we have more important things to worry about—namely that Carrie is on the verge of a mental breakdown.

See, the thing is that even though The Amy's' prank was totally lame and the kind of thing that any first-grader could have thought up, Carrie was majorly traumatized. I didn't even see her until we all got on the bus to go home. And she didn't want to talk about what happened.

She didn't want to talk about anything, as a matter of fact.

After the bus dropped her off, Jordan told me that he saw her in the infirmary after sixth period. He figured that she spent the rest of the day in there, waiting for her clothes to dry.

Just thinking about that makes me want to plant a very large atomic bomb in Amy Anderson's locker. . . .

Anyway.

I think the reason Carrie was so sketched out in the first place was because of the timing of the thing. It couldn't have happened at a worse moment. Carrie was so psyched. I mean, she was obviously embarrassed by Ms. Lloyd's announcement. But I knew she was kind of happy about it, too. She was blushing, but she was also smiling. She had even forgiven Jordan for taking the story in the first place.

Now I have a feeling that Carrie will never enter another story in a contest. I know how her mind works. She is a little paranoid. Knowing her, she won't get up in front of a crowd again for as long as she lives. After all, there's always that chance that people will bombard her with Jell-O cubes or rotten apple cores.

Or that The Amys will come rushing up behind her to spray her butt with water.

See? Now she actually has a reason to be paranoid. Or at least she thinks she does.

And that's what stinks most of all.

Eleven

Even though the rain had cleared and the late afternoon sunlight was streaming through her bedroom window, Alex couldn't bring herself to go outside and ride her skateboard. All she could do was sit on her unmade bed and stare at the phone. She'd been trying to figure out whether or not to call Carrie ever since she'd gotten home.

But what could she possibly say? Carrie knew the truth as well as she did: The Amys weren't going to make a fool out of her just *once*. Nope, they were going to come to the reading, too—to do it all over again.

Jeez. What was Carrie going to do? She couldn't back out of the reading now—not after Miss Lloyd's announcement. That would be even *more* humiliating.

Alex shook her head. If only she hadn't told Jordan about the story. . . .

Brinnng!

She sat up with a start. The phone was ringing. Maybe it was Carrie. She hesitated—then picked it up before the second ring.

"Hello?" she breathed.

"Hey—it's Jordan."

"Jordan." Alex sighed. "What's up?"

"Is this a bad time?" he asked.

"No, no," she mumbled. "It's just that . . . I was kind of hoping you might have been Carrie. I've been thinking about calling her." She paused. "Have *you* spoken to her?"

"No," he said. "But I think I figured out a way to keep The Amys from coming to the Cheshire Cat Bookstore this Sunday."

Alex raised her eyebrows. *"You did?"* she asked.

"Yeah," he said. "See, what happened today in the lunchroom made me realize something. None of this would have even *happened* if it wasn't for me. And I—"

"Jordan, it *wasn't* your fault," Alex interrupted. "Seriously. *Don't* feel guilty. The Amys were getting us back for last week. It had nothing to *do* with you—"

"No, just let me finish," Jordan insisted. "The thing is, I completely understood what

Carrie was going through. Remember that time in the sixth grade when my brother Mark yanked my sweatpants down to my ankles in front of the girls' soccer team?"

Alex swallowed, blushing slightly. How could she forget *that*? "Um . . . barely," she lied. There was no point in making him live through *that* pain all over again.

"Well, anyway, the prank today got me thinking," he said. "*I've* been looking for a way to get Mark back ever since the sixth grade. And I know Carrie must be feeling the exact same way about The Amys. So it's time to kill two birds with one stone. Or six, really."

Alex's eyes narrowed. "What are you getting at?"

He took a deep breath. "I was thinking we could use my brothers the same way you guys used Matt last week. You know, with the whole crush thing? I mean, I *know* Amy has a crush on Mark. Or at least she did last year. And if we could somehow convince Mel and Aimee that two large moronic senior twins had crushes on *them*—namely Peter and Paul—I bet we could get all *three* of The Amys and my three brothers at once. I could set up some sort of phony date for them on Sunday, during Carrie's reading."

Alex almost laughed. That sounded *nuts*. *"How?"* she asked.

"Well, um—I'm still working on that," he admitted. "But I was thinking we could somehow convince my brothers that Mel and Aimee are Amy's older sisters."

Alex started shaking her head. "Jordan—how are you gonna convince Peter and Paul that Mel and Aimee are older than Amy?" she asked. "It's impossible. Besides, you forgot a sort of crucial fact of life. Mel is Chinese. There's no *way* she could pass for one of Amy's sisters."

"But what if they don't actually *see* each other until the last possible minute?" Jordan asked hopefully. He sounded as if he were trying to convince himself as much as he was trying to convince her. "What if they only talk to each other on the phone?"

"I don't know," Alex murmured. "It sounds like a long shot."

"Well—it's a long shot I'm willing to risk," Jordan stated.

Alex lay back on her bed. "Do you honestly think you can pull it off?" she asked, mostly just to humor him.

"Probably not," he replied. "But in a way it doesn't even matter. As long as I tie them up on Sunday long enough for Carrie to give her reading, then I'll be all set."

Alex hesitated. "So you wouldn't even go to the bookstore?" she asked.

"If *I* go, The Amys go," he said grimly. "And somebody's gotta do *something*."

"I don't know," she murmured. "Carrie would be really bummed if you didn't make it."

"She'll get over it, though," Jordan said. "This is *important*, Alex. I mean, I thought that nothing bad could have possibly come out of entering a story in a contest. But I was totally wrong. It's like . . . it's like the *least* I can do."

Alex didn't say anything for a moment. The idea sounded totally crazy . . . but she had to hand it to Jordan—it was gutsy. No, it was more than gutsy; it was practically suicidal. If all *three* of his oversized brothers found out he was playing a trick on them . . . well, she shouldn't dwell on the "what ifs." Jordan's mind was made up. So at this point, he needed all the encouragement he could get.

"Are you gonna tell Carrie?" she finally asked.

"No way," he stated. "It would just make her feel all guilty and self-conscious—like she wasn't sticking up for herself or something. You know how she is. She likes to handle her problems herself." He paused. "Alex, you have to *swear* you won't tell her I'm trying anything."

"I won't, I won't," Alex promised. She sighed again. "Well, I guess all I can say at this point is good luck."

"Thanks," Jordan groaned. "I'm gonna need it."

Skyler Foley's Confession

I'm really confused. I know, I know—that's pretty normal for me. But still...

I actually feel <u>bad</u> for Jordan Sullivan.

Bizarre, huh?

Maybe I should explain. When Alex told me what Jordan was going to do to The Amys (or what he was going to <u>try</u> to do, anyway) I was totally shocked. And psyched, too, of course. Jordan is going <u>way</u> above and beyond the call of duty. It's probably the coolest thing he's ever done.

But I'm also sad. I'm sad that Jordan is going to miss out on Carrie's reading. And I'm not sad for myself. I'm sad for <u>him.</u>

You see, <u>I</u> have a little experience with missing out. I know what it's like. It's probably one of the worst feelings in the world. Like this one time last year, everybody went on a field trip to the Seattle Aquarium except me. I couldn't go because my parents had forgotten to sign my permission slip.

So I sat home and cried. I never told Carrie

or Alex—but it's true. I was in the seventh grade, but I cried like a baby over a lousy trip to the aquarium.

I don't know if Jordan's going to cry or anything—but I _do_ know he's going to feel like garbage. And not because The Amys will hate him and his brothers will totally stomp all over him. He's going to feel like garbage because _we're_ all going to be at Carrie's reading—and _he_ isn't.

It's not really fair at all.

But I understand why he wants to do this prank. Jordan would feel totally responsible if The Amys ruined the reading. He wouldn't _be_ responsible—but he would feel that way. And I have a little experience with that kind of feeling, too. Like when I convinced Carrie to go to Amy's house that day, _I_ felt responsible....

Anyway, I'm going to make sure that somebody videotapes the reading so that Jordan will have a chance to see it. It's the least we can do.

I just hope I can keep the whole thing a secret from Carrie until then. Keeping secrets isn't really my specialty.

Carrie's Countdown
to Disaster

TEN...
THURSDAY AFTERNOON

Carrie notices two curious items on her oak desk when she gets home from school. One is a note from her mom. The other is a brand-new laptop computer:

It was on sale, honey, so I couldn't resist! It's got all kinds of neat features—like a built-in modem and fax. You can send notes to all your friends instead of talking on the phone! I'll show you how to use it when I get home. Oh—by the way, I won't be here for dinner. You can heat up that leftover veal loaf in the fridge. Enjoy!

Love, Mom

NINE...
THURSDAY EVENING

Carrie dumps the computer into the back of her closet and closes the door.

EIGHT...
THURSDAY NIGHT

There's a knock on Carrie's door. Carrie's mom wants to help set up Carrie's computer. Carrie politely refuses, saying that she's too tired. Of course, she isn't tired at all. She's paralyzed with fear. She's *really* going to be doing this reading. The Amys are *really* going to be there. So she asks her mom if they can deal with the computer some other time. Right now, it's in her closet for safekeeping.

SEVEN...
FRIDAY MORNING

Carrie arrives at school to find that The Amys have postered the halls with homemade flyers, encouraging everyone to go to the Cheshire Cat Bookstore on Sunday.

SIX...

Carrie checks into the infirmary with a stomachache. Nurse Simmons remarks worriedly that Carrie has been feeling sick to her stomach almost every day this week. Maybe she should go home. Before calling for a cab, however, Nurse Simmons congratulates Carrie for winning the fiction contest. Carrie nearly loses her breakfast right there in the office.

FIVE...
FRIDAY MIDMORNING

Upon returning home, Carrie sits at her typewriter and begins to compose a list of possible ways to avoid the crisis but doesn't get past: (1) Alter my appearance and leave town.

FOUR...
FRIDAY EVENING

Carrie receives anxious calls from both Sky and Alex. Why was she rushed home in a cab this morning? Is she really sick? Will

96

she be able to do the reading? No—she's not really sick. Well, not at the moment, anyway. And yes—she'll be able to do the reading. But she instructs the two of them to get started on her funeral arrangements as soon as possible. She's pretty sure she won't live past Sunday. Not if The Amys can help it.

THREE...
SATURDAY MORNING

In a panic, Carrie realizes she hasn't even come up with an excuse to be out of the house on Sunday. She asks her mom if she can study for the math test with Sky.

TWO...
FIVE MINUTES LATER

Carrie calls Sky. Can she bum a ride to the reading? It's kind of important . . .

ONE...
SUNDAY NOON

The Foleys' beat-up old van arrives at the Mersels' house. The entire Foley family is present. Even Sky's little brother, Leif, is coming along. As the van pulls away, Sky tells Carrie that they brought their video camera to tape the entire event. Carrie ponders throwing the van door open, diving out onto Pike's Way, and making a run for it.

KA-BOOM!
SUNDAY, 12:50 P.M.

The Foleys drop Carrie off in front of the Cheshire Cat, then park. For several minutes, Carrie remains on the sidewalk. She's too terrified to move. Finally, she forces herself to walk through the door. There *is* no escape. Unless she passes out, of course. After all, it's kind of hard to read out loud when you can't breathe.

Twelve

So this is it, Carrie said to herself miserably. *This is where I'm gonna go down in history as "The World's Biggest Loser."*

The place was *packed*.

"Carrie—is that you?" a woman's voice called from somewhere in the crowd.

Carrie was too distraught to utter any kind of sound—let alone respond to that question. All she could do was gape at the mass of people milling around the store. She recognized at least a dozen kids from Robert Lowell. Some of them were kids she barely even *knew*. Why had they even come? To watch her make a fool out of herself?

Her eyes wandered to a little platform with one single chair, right in front of an enormous window that looked out onto Second Avenue.

A terrible, sinking sensation settled over her. Was that chair for *her*? She'd be such an easy target up there. She scanned the room again. At least The Amys weren't here yet.

"Carrie?"

The voice was much closer now. Carrie saw a woman pushing her way through the crowd and waving. She looked about thirty—tall with long, curly brown hair and little round glasses. She was wearing this long, cool black dress. As she drew closer, Carrie saw that she wore really cool silver rings on her hands, too. Carrie just stared. Who *was* she? She looked like she stepped right out of an Alternative Nation video.

"That is *you*, isn't it?" the woman asked with a smile.

At once, Carrie recognized her voice.

"Uh . . . Ms. Wallace?" she asked, completely caught off guard.

"Please," she said, laughing. "Call me Peggy. 'Ms. Wallace' makes me feel like an old lady."

Carrie had to laugh, too. She couldn't believe it. For a moment, she even forgot about The Amys. She had imagined Peggy Wallace to be this prim and proper bookish type—like Ms. Lloyd. In fact, she had been expecting everything about this bookstore to be a lot more . . . well, grown-up.

But now that she really took a good look at the place, she saw that the atmosphere was totally casual and laid-back. Maybe it also had to do with the fact that there were more comic books and magazines on display than actual *books*.

"How did you know it was me?" Carrie asked.

Peggy smiled. "Lucky guess. I just met your friend Alex. She told me that you dyed your hair black. I love it, by the way."

"Uh, thanks," Carrie mumbled. She looked at the floor. *Wow,* she thought. No adult except Brick had ever complimented her on her hair before. This place *was* cool.

"Anyway, I'm really glad you could come," Peggy said.

Carrie nodded. "Me too," she said—and for a brief moment, it was true. For the first time since maybe Thursday, she actually found herself relaxing. Not much, of course—but a tiny little bit. But then the panic kicked back in. . . .

"Hey, George, come over here!" Peggy called. "Carrie's here!"

Carrie looked up. A guy with a beard and a ponytail headed toward them.

"So this is the child prodigy, huh?" he asked wryly, extending a hand. "Nice to meet you."

"Um . . . you too," Carrie said, giving his hand a quick shake. "I think child prodigy is pushing it a little . . ."

He laughed. "Don't be so modest. But you know, I have to tell you something. I wasn't expecting your story to win. I mean, your friend was very confident about your talent, but . . ."

Carrie didn't follow. "My friend?"

"Yeah. You know, the one who gave me your story."

"Oh . . . Jordan." Carrie nodded.

"Well, he's clearly your biggest fan," George continued.

"Yeah, I guess so," Carrie mumbled. Where *was* Jordan, anyway? Her eyes roved over the crowd again. She could see Alex and Sam standing near a table loaded with cider and cookies, but Jordan was nowhere in sight.

"Hey—speaking of fans, it looks like some more people are arriving," Peggy said. "This is so great! You really got a big turnout."

Don't thank me—thank The Amys, Carrie thought glumly.

The Foleys were stumbling through the door, with Sky leading the pack. Mr. Foley was struggling to keep the camera tripod balanced on his shoulder and hold onto Leif's hand at the same time. Sky's mom's arms were loaded down with the rest of the camera equipment.

"Is it okay if we set up this stuff somewhere?" Mr. Foley panted. Beads of sweat dampened his forehead.

"Of course!" Peggy said. "Here, follow me. . . ."

She quickly led him through the crowd, with Leif and Mrs. Foley following close on their heels. "Good luck, Carrie!" Mr. Foley called over his shoulder.

"Thanks," Carrie called back. *I'm gonna need more than luck.*

"So, are you all ready to read?" Sky asked eagerly.

Carrie shrugged. Suddenly her heart lurched. *Oh no . . .*

"What is it?" Sky asked anxiously.

"I . . . uh, don't have my story." She shot a terrified look at George. "That copy was—"

"Don't worry," he said, patting her shoulder. "Everything's okay. I have the original safely locked up in my desk."

Carrie's head drooped. Her heart was still thumping. She supposed she should have been relieved, but in a way, she wasn't. In a way, she was secretly kind of hoping the story was lost forever. That way, she wouldn't have to go through with the reading at all.

"Hey, don't *worry*," Sky soothed, grinning. "Everything's gonna work out great."

Carrie just shook her head. "You know that's not true," she moped.

George patted her shoulder one last time. "Of *course* it is," he said. "Listen, I'm gonna go get the story right now, so you can look it over one last time."

Carrie nodded. "Thanks a lot," she breathed—but she was thinking: *Yeah, one last time before The Amys attack.*

She watched as George scurried through the crowd. As far as she could see, The Amys still hadn't showed.

And neither had Jordan.

Where *was* he, anyway?

Thirteen

"I'm telling you, man—I *heard* them talking about you guys," Jordan was saying. "I swear! If you don't believe me, just call them."

Paul's dull blue eyes narrowed. Jordan couldn't help but notice that his brother looked even more apelike than usual.

"Don't try to pull one over on me," Paul warned.

Jordan sighed. He had been sitting at the kitchen table with Paul for what seemed like *years*, trying to convince him to call Amy Anderson's house—but Paul just kept on repeating the same stupid threats, over and over again. And it was already almost one o'clock. The Amys might have already assumed he wouldn't call. They might have already left for the Cheshire Cat. . . .

"Why should I believe you?" Paul grunted.

Jordan shrugged. "Well, either I'm lying and you beat the crap out of me, *or* Mel Anderson really wants to meet you. Either way, you can't lose."

Paul just stared at him.

Why didn't I think of a plan B? Jordan wondered desperately. Until now, he actually thought he had a semidecent chance of pulling this whole thing off.

Last night, he'd gotten Sam to call Amy—pretending to be Mark. Amazingly, Amy had bought the whole act, owing to Sam's miraculous ability to imitate anyone on the planet. The trap had been set. "Mark" had promised Amy that his older brother Paul would be calling on Sunday no later than twelve forty-five. But now, it looked as if everything would fall apart.

"Which one's Mel?" Paul asked for the fourth time.

"The *middle* one," Jordan groaned. "I told you. You don't remember? Blond? Real thin? Nineteen? She goes to Seattle State. I can't believe you don't remember. She was only two years ahead of you. She remembers *you*." Jordan had repeated the lie so many times that he was almost starting to believe it himself.

"All right," Paul stated. He jerked a beefy hand across the table. "Gimme the number."

Finally. Jordan reached into his jeans pocket, pulling out a crumpled piece of paper with Amy Anderson's number on it. Paul snatched the paper out of his hand and marched over to the wall phone by the refrigerator.

"You're welcome," Jordan muttered.

Paul slowly dialed the number with his stubby forefinger.

For a moment, the two of them just stared at each other.

Then Paul blinked. "Uh, yes, hello," he said into the phone. "Is Mel there, please?"

There was a pause. "Thanks." Paul grinned slightly.

Jordan raised his hands, as if to say "I told you so." He tried to mask the flood of relief that was coursing through his body. Obviously, The Amys *hadn't* left yet. So there was still a chance . . .

Paul was now totally oblivious to Jordan's presence. "Mel?" he asked. "Uh, hi. This is Paul Sullivan."

Jordan's smile widened.

"Not bad," Paul said. "How you doin'?"

Nice line, Jordan thought sarcastically.

Paul's eyes narrowed. "You sound . . . I don't know. Younger than I expected."

Uh-oh. Jordan's stomach instantly squeezed into a tight knot.

But then Paul laughed. "Nah . . . it's cool. I didn't mean any offense or anything. So, uh, I was thinking, maybe my brothers and I could get together with you guys this afternoon."

Jordan held his breath.

"The sooner the better," Paul said with a big, idiotic smile. There was another long pause. "Great. I'll see you then." He placed the phone back on the hook.

"See?" Jordan said, sighing. He grinned broadly.

"Shut up, twerp," Paul muttered. "Peter! Mark!" he yelled. "Get your butts down here. We got dates!"

Jordan bit the inside of his cheek to keep from laughing. *We got dates!* Yup, they sure did. Dates with three stuck-up thirteen-year-olds. He couldn't wait to see the expression on Paul's face when he saw who Mel Anderson really was. . . .

Paul headed for the front hall.

"Where are you going?" Jordan asked nonchalantly.

"The Andersons' house," he said. There was a loud pounding on the stairs as Peter and Mark dashed down to meet him. "Don't bother coming along," he added.

"Don't worry, I won't," Jordan mumbled. *At least, not where you can see me.*

The front door slammed.

Jordan rubbed his palms together, chuckling to himself. He'd done it. He'd actually *done* it. Of course, that also probably meant he had less than twenty-four hours to live, but it was worth it. Sometimes, incredibly enough, it paid to have three brothers whose combined IQ was less than his own shoe size.

Now all he had to do was convince his dad to take him back to the Cheshire Cat Bookstore—with a little detour past Amy Anderson's house.

And compared to the rest of the plan, that would be a piece of cake.

Fourteen

"Come on," Sky kept saying. "Cheer up. You're gonna do fine."

Carrie just wished she would shut up. It was ridiculous. The more Sky talked, the worse she felt. She couldn't *believe* Jordan hadn't shown. Was he mad at her or something? Was he trying to insult her in some way?

"Alex!" Sky called. "Sam! Come here!"

Carrie looked up. Alex and Sam were still munching on oatmeal cookies. She shook her head. At least everyone *else* had come. She watched as the two of them made their way through the crowd, spilling crumbs and making general slobs of themselves. Carrie couldn't help but notice that they had dressed up for the occasion. Sam was wearing a button-down shirt that was actually tucked in. He had a belt, too. And Alex had traded in her usual green cap and frayed black jeans for a sweater and khakis.

Man, oh man. In a way, their nice clothes made her even *more* depressed. Sam and Alex had gotten all decked out for the occasion, but Jordan hadn't even bothered to *come.*

There's no way I can go through with this, she suddenly said to herself. *I just can't do it. I'm too bummed out. I'm too nervous. . . .*

"Rrrud Rrruck," Sam said with his mouth full.

Carrie managed a halfhearted smile. "Uh . . . what was that?"

He forced himself to gulp, then smiled. "Good luck."

"Oh," she murmured. "Thanks."

"Break a leg," Alex added.

Carrie hung her head. "That sounds like something Jordan would say," she muttered. "Where *is* he?" she wondered out loud.

Alex, Sky, and Sam exchanged glances.

Carrie looked at them. She drew in her breath sharply. "Is he afraid I'm still mad at him? Did he stay at home?"

Sky looked at her shoes. "No, not at *home . . .*"

Nobody said another word. Now all *three* of them were looking at their shoes.

111

"All right, what is going on here?" Carrie demanded. "If you guys know something . . ."

"He's with The Amys," Alex mumbled.

"Please," Carrie groaned. "Now is *not* the time. Seriously. Where is he?"

"She *is* being serious," Sam said. "He's with The Amys. Well, not *with* them exactly. More like . . . *near* them."

Carrie blinked. A strange tingling sensation had started creeping up her spine. Something very *odd* was going on—and she wasn't sure what. She only knew it was making her even *more* nervous than she'd been before, if such a thing were possible.

"He's making sure The Amys are occupied," Sky said.

Carrie couldn't seem to process Sky's words. They made absolutely no sense. "He's *what?"*

"He came up with this whole elaborate scheme to prevent The Amys from coming here today," Alex said. "His brothers think they have dates with Amy Anderson's older sisters. Amy, Aimee, and Mel think they have dates with Jordan's brothers. They're all meeting at Amy Anderson's

112

house today. That way we could be sure that The Amys wouldn't be here to ruin your reading."

Carrie's jaw hung open slackly. She was still too stunned to grasp the full meaning of what Alex had just told her. For some reason, she could think of only one response.

"Jordan's brothers are going to *kill* him," she whispered.

"Yup," Sam said simply.

Right at that moment, George came running up. "Here you go," he said, handing her the story.

"Uh . . . thanks," she croaked.

"I guess we should sit down," Sky said. Her face brightened. "Good luck!"

"Yeah, knock 'em dead, Carrie," Alex added.

Sam gave her a thumbs-up.

Carrie watched as the three of them began to jockey for sitting space on the rug. She was still in a state of shock. Was it really time? She couldn't get up there and read. She felt woozy, as if someone had clobbered her over the head with a large mallet.

"I figured we'd get started in about five minutes," George said. He glanced around the room. "Unless there's anybody else you want to wait for. Hey—where are your parents?"

Parents?

"Uh—they, uh, they couldn't make it," she stammered, instantly snapping out of her stupor. "They, um, had to go out of town on a . . . uh, a business trip. There was no way they could change it."

"Oh . . . that explains the video camera," George said. "Well, I'll give you a few minutes to look over the story." He pointed to Peggy, who was standing off to one side next to Mr. Foley and his tripod. "Just let Peggy know whenever you're ready."

Carrie swallowed. She tried to match his smile. "Okay," she breathed.

"Don't worry," he called cheerfully, sitting down. "You're gonna do great."

Carrie nodded. But all she could think about at that moment was: *"That explains the video camera."* No. The only thing that explained the video camera was that her *friend's* parents cared more about her life than her *own* parents.

Well, there was no point in dwelling on *that*. Her parents knew she won the contest. But instead of being enthusiastic, they'd forbidden her to do the reading. And even if they had given her permission, Carrie doubted they would have come to watch her read. They probably would have found a convenient excuse to do something they really cared about—like watch TV or buy a new laptop computer.

But she had her friends. And her friends *cared*.

She laughed once in spite of herself.

They really *did* care. Jordan cared so much that his face was probably getting mashed to a fine pulp right now. He was doing that for *her*. But why? What had she done to deserve it?

"Carrie?" Peggy called.

A hush fell over the crowd. By now, everybody had carved a space for themselves on the floor. The lone chair on the little platform towered over the sea of their expectant faces.

"Ready?" Peggy asked.

Carrie paused. Was she ready? Until about thirty seconds ago, she'd been tempted to bolt from the store. But now, amazingly enough, her nervousness began to subside. The Amys wouldn't be coming.

And if Jordan had mustered the courage to confront The Amys *and* his brothers at one time, then she could muster the courage to face this crowd.

A swell of confidence billowed up inside her. Yup, she was going to do this. She gripped the story tightly in her hands and marched to the platform. She was determined. She was going to give the best reading she could possibly give. She was going to make this worthwhile for all of them: Sky, Alex, Sam, the Foleys, . . . and Mr. Wagner and Matt, too. Even Ms. Lloyd and Nurse Simmons.

But most especially, she would do it for Jordan.

"Ladies and gentlemen," Peggy announced as Carrie took a seat on the platform. "Thank you for coming to the first annual Cheshire Cat Young Writers' Contest. It is my great pleasure to introduce to you our winner, Carrie Mersel. . . ."

Fifteen

I

"Thanks for the lift," Jordan mumbled to his father gratefully. He settled back in the front passenger seat and opened the window a crack as the car sped down Pike's Way. It was a beautiful, clear Sunday afternoon. The cold wind felt good against his face. He hadn't realized he'd been sweating so much during his little conversation with Paul.

"It's no problem," Mr. Sullivan said, clutching the wheel. "I just wish you would have told me about this reading at the bookstore sooner." He sighed. "I can't guarantee we'll make it, either. Hopefully I won't get a ticket."

Jordan nodded. "Well, don't go *too* fast." He swallowed. "Oh, yeah—there's just one more thing. Would you, uh, mind swinging by Pacific Drive on our way out?"

His father frowned slightly. "Why?"

A brief grin crossed Jordan's face. "I just wanna check on something. It'll only take a second."

II

The afternoon had turned cold and damp by the time Alice, Suzanne, and Mercedes climbed the hill to the mansion. Mercedes wished she were somewhere else— anywhere. A bitter wind blew from the north. The entire landscape was bathed in a colorless gray, like the stone of the mansion's walls.

"This place is even more amazing in the daytime," Alice said with a shiver.

"Yeah," Suzanne agreed. "It's a killer."

Mercedes kept quiet. She still couldn't believe she was even here. But her two friends were clearly convinced that nothing was wrong. Nothing at all . . .

At first, as Carrie had been reading, she'd had a hard time even getting her lips to form the syllables. Her mouth and lips and tongue felt as if they were made of sandpaper. The typed pages were quivering in her hands.

What am I even doing here? She kept asking herself.

But she had to stay focused. Which meant, of course, she could *not* sneak a little peek at the audience again. She'd done that once and nearly had a heart attack right on the spot.

"Come in, come in," Alexis called, appearing out of the darkened hall. "I'm so glad you could make it."

Alice and Suzanne immediately stepped inside. Only Mercedes hesitated.

"Come on, Mercedes," Alexis called with a laugh.

Every part of Mercedes's body seemed to be screaming at her: "Turn back!" But she forced her feet to move.

"Where are we going?" she asked.

"To the kitchen," Alexis replied.

Mercedes had never been to the kitchen. In fact, she had never been in this part of the mansion at all.

"This house is so big," Suzanne murmured.

"Where are Krystle and Fallon?" Mercedes wondered out loud. She glanced over her shoulder behind her--but all she could see was a shadowy nothingness.

"They're waiting for us," Alexis said.

III

As soon as the car turned onto Pacific Drive, Jordan started smiling. There they were: three blond meatheads standing in the doorway of Amy Anderson's enormous, supermodern white house.

"Jordan, why are you checking up on Peter, Paul, and Mark?" his father asked, slowing the car as they approached. He shook his head, smirking. "You're not spying on their dates, are you?"

"Nope," Jordan said nervously. The car was going a little *too* slow. If any one of them turned around right now, they would see Jordan right there. "I, uh, just wanted to make sure I gave them the right directions. They didn't know how to get here."

His father cocked an eyebrow. "They didn't?"

"Nope. We can go now. Better step on it."

His father shook his head, sighing, but he sped up. The car whizzed passed Amy Anderson's house, unnoticed.

"You know, Jordan," Mr. Sullivan said, "sometimes you can be one weird kid . . ."

But Jordan wasn't listening. He was staring over his shoulder, right at the most wonderful, satisfying sight he had ever seen in his life.

It was the befuddled look on Paul's face as Mel Eng opened the door.

IV

At that moment, Mercedes noticed a light ahead. Alexis pushed open the door, and Mercedes found herself in an enormous, brilliantly lit kitchen. It was the largest kitchen she had ever seen--with a wood-burning stove and countless white cabinets.

Krystle and Fallon were sitting at
the kitchen table.

It was only then that Mercedes
noticed the floor.

The floor with a black-and-white
checkerboard pattern.

She gasped.

"What is it?" Alexis asked.

She shook her head. She couldn't
speak. She felt as if she were
standing outside a thick and
impenetrable window, watching
helplessly as her two best friends
approached the table where Krystle
and Fallon were sitting. . . .

Carrie had gradually become aware that
the crowd was growing increasingly
quiet—until finally, they were silent.

At the beginning of the reading, people
had chuckled or mumbled or made little
noises depending on what was going on in
the story. But now there was nothing. It was
as if the entire room was holding its breath.

Carrie felt a little spark of excitement
shoot through her. The people in this room
were hanging on her every word.

Words *she* had written.

And as she plowed further, she began to fill the silence with her own voice—raising it to a shout, lowering it to a whisper—throwing herself into the story. Incredibly enough, it was actually *fun*.

She couldn't believe she had ever been so nervous to get up in front of a crowd in the first place. The dryness in her mouth was gone. After a while, she was hardly even conscious that there *was* an audience. All of her previous worries and fears had slipped away. In a weird way, she felt as if the characters were real, living people. It was as if, for this one moment, they had come magically to life.

Krystle and Fallon suddenly slumped to the floor.

Mercedes took a step back. "What's happening?" she hissed. She shot a horrified look at Alexis, who had clamped her own hand over her mouth. Her eyes were wide in silent terror.

"Surprised?" Alice asked, smiling wickedly.

Mercedes shook her head. This

---

was Alice, her best friend. But that glint in her eye was the glint of a total stranger. Mercedes took another step back--but she couldn't go any further. She had struck a wall. There was no escape.

"The people of Stony Brook have had just about enough," Suzanne said. She sprung forward and wrapped a handkerchief around Alexis's mouth, then pulled a rope from her own pocket and tied Alexis's hands behind her back.

"Enough of what?" Mercedes gasped.

"Enough of people with evil powers," Suzanne whispered. "This town is too small for secrets."

Mercedes's eyes remained fixed to Alexis as Alice wrapped a tight handkerchief around Mercedes's mouth. The fabric burned roughly against her lips and tongue. But that brief sting paled in compari- son to the searing pain of the rope that bound her hands behind her back.

And then Mercedes saw a flash of metal.

A muted cry escaped her throat.

Alice had brought a knife to Mercedes's neck. "You're just like Alexis," she whispered.

Like Alexis? Mercedes thought wildly. And then she knew. No wonder she had sensed something strange about Alexis.

Alexis was a psychic, too. And the whole town of Stony Brook had known.

"Time to meet your maker," Alice whispered. The cold metal of the blade remained pressed against Mercedes's neck, digging into her flesh.

Alice threw open the back door.

It was then Mercedes saw the most gruesome sight she had ever seen in her whole life.

She saw all the people of Stony Brook . . . standing in front of a raging wall of fire.

The End

Sixteen

The room exploded with applause.

Carrie jumped at the sound.

"*Car-rie, Car-rie, Car-rie,*" Matt started chanting.

She blushed. Everyone had pushed themselves to their feet. The sound of the clapping swelled. Carrie couldn't believe it. They were giving her a standing ovation. *Her.* Even in all her wildest fantasies about this day, she had never imagined *this.* Then again, most of her fantasies about this day had been nightmares involving The Amys.

Peggy stepped up onto the platform. Slowly, the applause began to die down.

"Before I say anything—I just want to let you know that the Cheshire Cat is not responsible for any nightmares that may occur as a result of this reading," she said dryly. "And now we get to the fun part. George?"

The crowd fell silent as George approached

the platform. He was carrying a small piece of green paper. Carrie stood up from the chair.

"It is my pleasure to present one gift certificate worth a hundred dollars off any purchase," George announced, handing her the paper and shaking her hand. "Congratulations. Hopefully one day we'll be seeing *your* name on these shelves."

Carrie's eyes bulged as she gazed at the certificate. Until she actually saw the amount of one hundred dollars printed in neat letters, she couldn't quite believe she had won a prize. She was absolutely speechless. "I—I . . . Thank you," she finally stuttered.

"No—thank *you*," he said.

"Speech!" somebody hollered.

A murmur of encouragement rippled through the crowd. Carrie's lips started quivering. She couldn't give a *speech*. If she opened her mouth, she might do something really dumb, like start bawling. Her eyes slowly swept across the room—across Sky and her parents, Alex and Sam, Matt and Mr. Wagner . . . until finally they came to rest on someone standing by the front door.

"Jordan!" she cried.

He must have just gotten here. He was doubled over and panting, but Carrie caught his smile beneath the mop of blond hair.

She took a deep breath. "I just have one thing to say. Well, actually I have two things to say." She laughed. "One is thank you. Thank you so much." She paused. "The other is that I really can't accept this prize money."

George and Peggy exchanged a puzzled glance.

"No, no—it's nothing bad or anything," Carrie went on. "It's just that there's someone who deserves it more. My story would have never even gotten entered in this contest if it wasn't for my friend, Jordan Sullivan." She waved the certificate at him. "He was the one who had faith in me. *He* deserves this a lot more than I do."

Everyone's head turned toward the door.

Jordan's eyes were wide. He was still breathing heavily—but he was grinning from ear to ear.

"So let's have a big round of applause for Jordan Sullivan," she said.

The sound of cheering filled the room once more as Carrie hopped off the platform and marched over to the front door.

"Why are you doing this?" Jordan whispered as she handed him the certificate.

"Because you deserve it," Carrie said simply.

He shook his head, gawking at the piece of paper. "Well, don't you at least want to split it or something?"

Carrie shook her head. "Nope. It's all yours." She flashed him a wry smile. "Of course, if I were you, I'd spend it as soon as I can. If what I hear is true, I don't know how much time you have left to enjoy it."

Jordan laughed once. "Yeah, I think you're right about that," he mumbled. "Luckily I escaped before any of them figured out what happened."

"Thank you so much, Jordan," she murmured. "I mean it. You didn't have to do what you did today."

He shrugged. "I know. But I wanted to."

Carrie didn't know what to say to that. And speechlessness was a problem she'd never had before. Normally, no matter *what* the circumstances, she always had some kind of witty comeback—some devastating one-liner that served as the last word. But the truth of the matter was that she was too overwhelmed to talk right now. She just hoped she wouldn't start weeping. After all, she had to maintain some sort of reputation. She wasn't *that* much of a softie.

"Thanks," she finally gasped.

The cheering faded once and for all.

"Well, we still have a lot of cider and cookies to finish up," Peggy announced from the platform. "So help yourselves. And thanks again for coming."

The crowd began to disperse. Scattered conversation filled the room. After one last shaky sigh, Carrie figured she could manage *some* reasonably intelligent conversation. But before she could, Sky, Alex, and Sam had surrounded her. She whirled around dizzily, trying to thank them all at once.

"Awesome," Sam pronounced.

"It was *more* than awesome," Alex cried. "You were incredible."

"I can't wait to watch it on video," Sky jabbered. "But Carrie, just so you know, Alex and I would never bound and gag and burn you in front of an angry mob."

Carrie laughed. "Gee, thanks, Sky. That's nice to know. I really appreciate that."

"Yeah, it's reassuring to know you're

not a homicidal maniac, Suzanne—I mean, Sky," Jordan smirked. "Now, I think I'm gonna go buy a hundred bucks worth of comic books."

Carrie watched as he disappeared into the crowd.

"You guys have to promise me something," she murmured to the other three.

"What's that?" Sky asked as they huddled around her.

"Whatever The Amys do to get him back for today, you gotta promise that we come up with something a million times better."

Seventeen

"I can't believe I really *sound* like that," Carrie groaned, covering her eyes with her hands. "And I look so . . . pale."

"Give me a break," Sky said. "You are not—"

"Shh!" Jordan hissed.

Carrie peeked through her fingers at the TV screen again. Why had she let them talk her into watching the videotape at her house? It was *way* too embarrassing. She really did look like the world's biggest loser. And contrary to what Sky said, she *was* pale. Especially since she was wearing all black.

"I'm gonna go get a snack," she announced, pushing herself off the living room carpet. "Anybody want anything?"

Nobody answered. Their eyes were all riveted to the screen.

"This is the best part," Alex whispered. "Of course, *they* weren't psychic. . . ."

Carrie hurried from the room. *That is the*

very last time I'm going to let myself be taped, she promised herself as she crossed through the front hall. *There's no way—*

She stopped.

There was a noise.

The front door latch was turning.

Carrie's pulse tripled in about two seconds. What was her mom doing here? She was going to be out shopping all day. And *Carrie* was supposed to be at Sky's house, studying for some math test. . . .

The door swung open.

Mrs. Mersel was right there. She jumped.

"Carrie!" she cried. She placed her hand over her chest. Then she took a deep breath and smiled, shaking her head. "You scared me, honey. What are you doing back so early? I thought you were going to be studying . . ." Her voice trailed off. "What is that sound?" she asked. "Are there people here?"

Carrie swallowed. "Um, well, a . . . uh, a few of us are watching TV," she stuttered lamely.

Mrs. Mersel pursed her lips. Without another word, she marched into the living room. Carrie immediately chased after her.

Uh-oh. This was going to be very, very difficult to explain. . . .

As soon as Alex saw Mrs. Mersel, she instantly reached for the TV remote.

"No, no," Mrs. Mersel said, folding her arms across her chest. "Leave it on."

Carrie's face sagged. This was not good. Not only had her mom caught her having a miniparty while she was gone, but the videotape proved she had lied about studying. No, she would definitely *not* let herself get taped again. Videotapes were always bad news. No wonder so many cop movies revolved around crucial videotape evidence.

The six of them remained perfectly still until the reading was over.

As soon as the crowd started applauding, Mrs. Mersel said, "Carrie, I'd like to have a word with you in the kitchen."

Oh, brother. Carrie hung her head. She slowly plodded after her mom. She would probably be grounded for the rest of her eighth-grade year. And after all the stress she had been through, this was just what she needed.

Mrs. Mersel closed the kitchen door behind them. "Carrie, I don't know what to make of what I just saw in there," she said.

Carrie sunk down into a chair at the kitchen table. "Look, Mom, I'm really sorry—"

"No, don't apologize," she interrupted. "I . . . I'm the one who should apologize."

Carrie's head shot up. "What?"

Mrs. Mersel nodded thoughtfully. "It's true. I see that you had a reason for lying to me. This reading, or whatever it was, was obviously very important to you. I should have seen that."

Carrie blinked. This was a majorly historical moment. For the second time in one day, she was at a total loss for words. Could it be that her mom was finally beginning to understand that, aside from her friends, writing was the most important thing in the world to Carrie?

A wistful smile formed on Mrs. Mersel's lips. "The point is, you obviously have a lot of talent. You're very good in front of a crowd. Very comfortable. I think it would be wonderful if you took some acting lessons."

Acting lessons?

Her mother's voice faded to a dull murmur as the air flowed out of Carrie's lungs. She felt like a deflating blimp.

Nope. It wasn't a historical moment at all. It was just the same old thing.

135

She should have known better than to get her hopes up like that. Once again, her mom had shown a glimmer of intelligence, then managed to miss the point entirely. Enroll her in a drama camp? What on earth was she thinking? It was just so . . . typical.

Carrie stared at her mother in disbelief.

"Maybe we could even enroll you in a drama camp," Mrs. Mersel was saying. "You could wind up on TV!"

Carrie opened her mouth to protest, but the only sound that came out was something between a snort and a laugh. From the TV room she could hear her friends laughing and joking as Jordan told Sky to rewind the tape so he could watch the reading again.

"I think I saw some acting schools advertised in one of my magazines." Her mother began rummaging through a stack of papers on the kitchen counter.

Carrie turned to leave the room, knowing her mother wouldn't even notice she was gone. She'd deal with avoiding drama camp later. One thing she knew for sure: The way her life was going, she'd never be lacking in inspiration for her stories.